D for Daisy

Nick Aaron

D for Daisy

The Daisy Hayes trilogy   I

ANOTHER IMPRINT PUBLISHERS

We roar all like bears, and mourn sore like doves: we look for judgment, but there is none; for salvation, but it is far off from us.

Isaiah 59:11

CONTENTS

I 1943: Murder over Berlin

That night, as they finally flew over the Dutch coast and
reached the North Sea, the crew on board D-Daisy became
very nervous. They were almost home, which should have
been a relief, but their skipper had been knocked out, and
Derek, the flight engineer, had taken over the controls. He
had never landed the aircraft before. He was now shouting
to his crewmates over the intercom.

"Rear-gunner! what do you say? Can the bomb-aimer
leave his guns now?"

"Yes, yes, I think so! We're still in range of the 'bandits',
but if they attack, it will *definitely* be from behind. So leave
them to the mid-upper and myself. We'll take care of them…"

"All right! So, Ken, get up here at once! I want you in the
flight engineer's seat pronto. And don't forget your chute;
we're still in bail-out readiness."

"Right! Coming!"

It took some time for Ken to disconnect his mask from
the oxygen supply, his flight helmet from the intercom lines,
and to extricate himself and his bulky flying suit from the
narrow nose-turret of the Lancaster. In the meantime Derek
called out to the wireless, who was stationed right next to the
first aid bed, "Wireless! how's the skipper doing? Can you feel
a pulse?"

"Dunno! I thought I felt something a while ago, but right
now I'm not sure. I'm still feeding some oxygen into his mask,

though..."

"Good! Can't you put a pocket mirror between his teeth or something; check if he's still breathing?"

"I don't *have* a pocket mirror, dammit! *Who's* got a pocket mirror on this kite? You don't fly all the way to Berlin to have a *shave*!"

"Hold your horses, for Chrissake!"

Derek and the crew were assuming that their skipper had been hit by flak, even though there was no visible wound. On their mission that night they had flown through several flak barrages, on the way out and coming back. It was inevitable on an op like this, deep into enemy territory. It meant you just had to fly on through exploding high altitude shells, with shrapnel bursting forth in all directions. And that in its turn always meant taking your chances in a deadly lottery where there were few winners. Tiny pieces of shrapnel would shoot right through the aircraft's skin and could hit an airman, acting like a dumdum bullet. Sometimes an unlucky chap took a direct hit, and his head or his chest just exploded. You heard gruesome stories. In this case, it seemed that the skipper had been badly injured by some freak splinter that had shredded a vital internal organ but hardly left a mark on the outside.

Meanwhile Ken had climbed from the bottom of the nose up to the flight deck, and connected himself to the engineer's station, to the right of the pilot's seat. "Bomb-aimer reporting, I'm at your station now, Derek, what do you want me to do?"

"Just read out the figures on every gauge on the panel in front of you. Start top left and go down row by row, like a book..."

Ken started to call out the figures.

"Faster! Faster! We haven't got much time!"

When he had finished reading out the figures, the bomb aimer asked anxiously, "What do you say, Derek, are we all

10

right?"

"Yes, the kite is sound, thank God. Fuel readings good. Hydraulics good. 'D for Daisy' can land."

"Yes, but can *you* land her?"

"I don't *know*, for crying out loud! I've never done it before. It's not that easy... Listen up, you chaps. I'm no good at yawing and breaking with the flaps to decrease our speed on the glide path. All that is just too tricky, as you can imagine. So we'll touch down at a much higher speed than we're used to, all right? It's going to be a rough landing... Now, wireless, I think it's time to call ahead and tell them this: skipper down; flight engineer in charge; emergency landing imminent; wounded man on board in critical state... All right?"

"Roger that! I'm on it."

As soon as the people manning flight control received the message, it was their turn to be nervous, even though for them it was all in a day's work. It wasn't unusual for a bomber to have dead or wounded crewmembers on board. And sometimes it was the skipper, the pilot himself, who had been knocked out. But of course there was no co-pilot on a bomber nowadays, for the simple reason that pilots were scarce. So it was the flight engineer who had to land the bomber, and that was the part that made everyone nervous. Landing such a behemoth for the very first time was a risky business and a frightening experience for all concerned.

Flight control had a slot prepared for the poor chaps; they needed a cleared runway; the other bombers would be put on hold while they landed. An experienced pilot on a direct link with the flight engineer on board the Lanc would try to talk him through the landing procedure. By the time D-Daisy approached her base, with the first intimations of dawn lighting up the horizon behind her, everything was in place.

So the Lancaster banged down onto the tarmac at high

speed, Derek immediately cut back the engines, raised the flaps as high as he could, and hit the brakes on the wheels of the landing gear as much as he dared. By some miracle the big machine kept steady and screeched to a standstill, just as the ambulance and the firefighters came rushing along. Then the crew sprang into action, lifted the inanimate body of their skipper off the first aid bed and clambered along the narrow gangway to the entry door at the back. The paramedics stood ready with a stretcher; the skipper was carried away immediately and the ambulance sped off.

Three of Daisy's friends sat yawning and grumbling at her kitchen table, in her small flat in Tufnell Park, on that same winter morning at half past seven.

"I'm not even awake yet," the first girl sighed.

"I should still be in bed, nicely warm and cosy," the second one added.

"I'm going to fail that exam anyway," the third one—who thought she was very wise—reflected. Her failing was not likely, but she believed in being pessimistic so that you could rely on the outcome exceeding your expectations.

At that moment Daisy returned briskly to the kitchen, and in the slightly hectoring tone that was typical of her, she exclaimed, "Cheer up, you girls! I can hear you grumbling all the way from the other end of the flat."

She was holding a plaster and papier-mâché model in her hands, which she had just retrieved from her bedroom. Her flat was strewn with these anatomical models, on loan from the professional training school: the skeleton, the muscles, the nervous system.

"Now let's see, what have we here? The muscles of the human torso..."

Daisy sat down at the table with the model in front of her, and with her head held high, not looking at her hands, she proceeded to remove the muscles of the chest and shoulders one by one, giving the name and the particulars of one part after another. Her three friends took turns looking up the answers in their anatomy manuals. She was rather impatient, and spurred them on relentlessly, running one muscle after the other by them.

"Gee whiz! This is uncanny, Daise," girl number one exclaimed, "your knowledge is already word-perfect!"

"Yes," Daisy admitted, "I believe I have it mapped in my mind pretty well..."

"It makes me wonder why we're here. You don't really need our help," girl number two remarked.

"Well, darling, as they don't have these anatomy books in Braille, I still need your eyes to check the answers for me, don't I? Besides, has it never occurred to you that in fact it is *I* who am helping *you* girls to memorize this stuff properly, not the other way round?"

"Be that as it may," girl number three grumbled, "*you* certainly don't need to worry about that exam!"

They continued to rehearse the muscles of the chest, Daisy taking them apart and then putting them back together. By the time the torso was complete again, Daisy suddenly remarked, "Why are these models always male, anyway? How are we supposed to treat a patient when there's a pair of *tits* in the way, right *here*... and *there*!" And she smiled, deadpan, her tiny teeth and the dimples in her cheeks imparting something childlike and innocent to her whole face.

The girls chuckled fondly. You could always rely on Daisy to have an original point of view on things. That was why they were so devoted to her. Of course you just couldn't refuse to help a blind girl, but in Daisy's case there was more than that involved. There had to be, as she was so demanding.

To start with, the girls were proud to be training for a profession, and a medical one at that, at St Mary's Hospital—

University of London, no less! Most girls didn't get any training at all, and the few who did mostly wanted to become nurses, but as physical-therapists-to-be, these girls felt far superior to the nurses-in-training. Daisy had once told them, "Nurses only do what the doctors say, and they want to marry one as soon as possible. As a physical therapist, at least, you're going to be your own man!"

That was another thing about Daisy: she was already married—to a bomber pilot, no less! Officially she was Mrs Ralph Prendergast. She had a flat of her own, the place where they were right now. She had sex each time her husband came home on leave. The glamour of that! And not only did she have sexual experience, but she was quite frank about it and willing to share her knowledge. "The proper terminology is 'making love'," she always corrected them. But as most of her fellow students were still virgins, the subject was shrouded in mystery and held endless fascination to them all.

Presently, at the kitchen table, girl number one was saying, "Oh, please, Daise, don't give me your Gorgon stare, everyone can make a mistake. Can I help it that the trapezius and the deltoid sound so similar to me?"

"Well I'm sorry, but I hate it when you sow confusion in my mind, that's all."

In a placating spirit, girl number three, who was new to the group, cried out, "It must be frustrating to be blind when you're so intelligent!"

But that only brought on another withering frown. "It must be frustrating to have eyes when you're so stupid!"

"Ouch! That hurts!"

The two other girls sniggered uncomfortably, and girl number two said, "Darling Daisy, sometimes you remind me of Dr Jekyll and Mr Hyde... Not that I've read the book, but you know what I mean."

The others laughed, "Yes, yes, we get the picture!"

Daisy laughed too. Then there was a knock at the door. "Who on earth could that be, this early?" the friends wondered aloud, but Daisy muttered, "I'm afraid I have a fair idea..."

When she opened her front door, she asked, "Major Mannings?"

"Good Lord! Mrs Prendergast, how can you tell?"

"Your uniform comes from the same cleaners as Ralph's, I can smell it. And of course, ever since Ralph started flying operations for you, I have been waiting for this moment..."

The man in front of Daisy had known in advance that the girl who would open the door of this poky little flat would be totally blind, but what was even more striking was her physical appearance and her self-assurance. She was exceptionally beautiful: tall, shapely and blonde.

Her hair formed a halo of wild blond curls around her head. Not the wavy perm of the forties, but a thicket of natural curls like Shirley Temple's. She looked extremely attractive in every respect, even rather sexy: hourglass silhouette; Hollywood glamour, so to speak—the major gulped. However, as she stood there in front of him, Daisy frowned fiercely, and the major was taken aback by her eyes. All one could see were ungainly slits, and what remained of her eyeballs reminded one of very unappetising scrambled eggs. As she frowned, the empty buttonholes of Daisy's atrophied eyes added something frightening and withering to her expression. That was what her schoolmates called "the Gorgon stare".

"Please come in, Major. I'll ask my friends to leave us alone now..."

A moment later, her three friends left the premises in a subdued silence. As graciously as she could, Daisy said, "Thanks for your help, girls, and good luck with that exam. I'm afraid I won't be taking it with you this time around..."

Then, when she had put aside the anatomical models

cluttering the kitchen table, and they had both taken a seat, Daisy said, "I guess you are here on account of Ralph?"

"Yes, alas, Mrs Prendergast..."

"Please, call me Daisy. I know I'm just a young girl to you... Tell me what happened."

"Well, *D for Daisy* did land safely at base last night, but Ralph's inanimate body was carried off to the sickbay, and later our Medical Officer sent back word that he was dead. There was nothing we could do..."

The girl said nothing. She just sat there at the kitchen table, frowning. The major peered intently at her face; with blind people, he supposed, it was not rude to do so as they couldn't tell. He now observed that her lower lip was trembling, observed the slight wobbling of her chin as she visibly fought back her tears. How long could she hold out before breaking down?

"Are you all right... erm... Daisy?"

The trembling stopped; she shook it off and pulled herself together.

"Yes... yes. Well, now you're here, you might as well take me back to the airbase at once!"

"Oh? I see! Yes, of course..."

"Have I just been ordered around by this girl?" Major Mannings wondered, as he and Daisy were driving out of London in his big black saloon car.

For Major Mannings this was an unusual notion. He was the Commanding Officer of a large RAF station in Essex; he was in charge of around seventy bombers, Lancasters, "real biggies" as he liked to call them. A pretty exciting and exacting job that put huge responsibilities squarely on a man's shoulders. And it had taken him longer than most to get to such a position, what with his RAF career stretching on endlessly after the Great War...

Lately he had suffered heavy losses, like all of Bomber

Command, because of the massive attacks on Berlin. One night after the other saw the loss of a fair number of bombers on their long-range operations deep into the Reich. All over the country many crews would fail to return to base.

Last night's operation had been all right, however, even rather successful. His men had been part of a bomber stream of 800 aircraft, but losses had been moderate. Perhaps the new system of dense flying formation was paying off after all. Still, one of his best pilots had been killed, even though his Lanc had made it back to base unharmed.

So, all was not well. Now that Ralph was dead, it was he himself, the CO of the airbase, who had to drive into London and go tell the widow about it. That was now the established procedure at his station, and it was the very same Ralph Prendergast who had insisted that it be so. "Wouldn't you agree, Sir, that it's the least you can do when one of us dies?" Such a well-bred young fellow... However, there had never been any question of taking the widow along to the airbase!

As they drove on through open country, Major Mannings marvelled at the blind girl sitting next to him. She was now wearing dark glasses, two simple black discs mounted in a wire frame, and she had a white bamboo cane by her side, and a brown leather handbag on her lap. But what was truly eerie about her was her total composure. Not a sob, not a sound, not a tear from her. On his way into London the major had dreaded and loathed the idea that once again, he was going to have to deal with a very young war widow who would break down completely when she heard the news he was bringing. But none of the usual spectacle with this one. No shrieks, no bawling, no throwing oneself on the ground and beating the floor with tiny fists. That had been a tremendous relief, of course, but it felt awkward all the same to be sitting next to this forbidding blind Sphinx now, who was still frowning fiercely, and to be driving back to the airbase in complete stillness...

17

At length the major couldn't help himself; he had to speak up. "I say, er, Daisy, you don't seem to cry easily, do you?"

"No, you're right, Sir. But believe me, if I could cry, I would."

They drove on for a while, then Daisy asked, "Did you see Ralph's body? Was he badly maimed?"

"I wouldn't know, I didn't see him, no..."

Daisy frowned some more. "How strange..."

"Well, you know, you get word from the Medical Officer and you just act on it: I didn't find it necessary to go and see the body as such."

"Well, *I* want to see it if I may. That is: touch it with my fingers, obviously."

"Oh yes, by all means! You will be brought to the morgue if you so wish, of course... So that is why you wanted to come with me... You know, it was Ralph himself who made sure that I myself, or one of my senior officers, should break the news to you in person..."

Then an idea struck the major. "I say, Daisy. Tonight we have another operation on; I'll be quite busy. So do you mind taking a train back to London when we're done? I can arrange for someone to escort you to the station... Or someone could drive you home?"

"No, not necessary. I can take the train on my own. There are so many kind and helpful people around. I will always find someone to help me on board, and even on a crowded train a seat is almost guaranteed..."

"Oh, splendid!"

And that is how Daisy ended up sitting on a hard chair in an office at the morgue in Great Dunmow, a small town near her dead husband's RAF station. The middle-aged official who received her marvelled at how beautiful this blind girl was—he even gulped. Then he said slowly, as if talking to a child, "Normally we would require of you, as the widow of the deceased, the painful duty of identifying your loved one. However, as you are blind..."

"Yes, yes, I know, I cannot legally identify Ralph. But believe me, I'll know it's him all the same. I only wish to touch his face. I want to hear and smell his absence, as it were. Exactly as normal people would say: I need to see him. So please, I beg you..."

The official picked up the phone and asked the morgue attendant to come and escort the lady, then they waited for his arrival in a deadly silence. The man just didn't know what to say to this blind girl with her dark glasses and her white cane. She was holding her handbag on her lap with one hand and had placed her little brown suitcase neatly on the floor next to her chair. She looked very young, awfully young for a war widow, like a little girl play-acting at being a grown-up. But a lot of the war widows he received in his office nowadays were like that.

When at last she was in the presence of Ralph's body, Daisy placed her fingertips on his face and started to stroke his features. It was Ralph all right, the great love of her life: the man she had been in love with since she had been sixteen, and had been married to for almost three years. She caressed his face softly, lovingly, for a long time. She started to cry. Silent and mucous tears issued sparingly from the hollows of her atrophied eyes and trickled slowly from under her dark glasses and down her cheeks. After a while she asked the attendant in an unsteady voice, "Excuse me, I'd like to touch the wounds. As I am blind, you understand, I can only know how my husband died by touch. Would you be kind enough to guide my hands to the wounds?"

"Certainly, Madam. Let me take away the shroud..."

There was a silence while the attendant drew back the sheet and started looking for the wounds. Daisy could hear that he was swallowing hard, probably on account of her, probably fighting back a few tears. After a moment he managed to mumble something about turning over the body, then there was a longer pause as he turned the corpse back and forth while still looking. Finally he gasped and said, "I really can't seem to find any wounds, Madam, I'm awfully sorry..."

"This is certainly very strange, isn't it?"

"I don't know. Now that I think of it, it does seem a bit strange, yes."

Daisy mulled this over, all the while probing the corpse with her fingertips, and finally asked, "You're the man who cleans the corpses, I take it? Did you ever before have an airman who died during an op and had no wounds?"

"No. Now that you ask: never, Madam."

"So when you washed Ralph's body, didn't it strike you as odd that he didn't have any?"

"Well, I didn't think of it at the time. I guess I was assuming that this young man was a civilian..."

"Oh no, this is Ralph all right. Pilot Officer Ralph Prendergast, he was the skipper on a Lancaster."

"Yes, Ralph Prendergast, that's what the label attached to his left toe also states. But no military rank, they must have forgotten to write it down at the station... Normally they also write down the rank."

While they were talking, Daisy's fingertips kept going up and down her dead husband's body, not even skipping the most intimate parts, which caused the attendant to swallow hard again. After a while the blind young women said, "Thank you ever so much for your patience, you've been a great help..."

Back in the morgue official's office, Daisy explained the situation to him. She made a conscious effort to sound subdued and deferential, a tone not natural to her, and asked if it would not be advisable to perform an autopsy on the deceased in order to determine the cause of death, "That is, assuming it hasn't been done already, of course."

"Well no. We don't normally order an autopsy on dead airmen. Surely you can understand why."

"Yes, but as it appears that my late husband has no wounds..."

"Well, first of all, we don't have a positive identification yet. Officially we don't know that this is your husband we're talking about."

"All right, I get that. I'll call my mother-in-law as soon as I can get to a phone. I assume a mother is entitled to identify her son?"

"Yes, yes, of course. But even so. As I said, we receive too many dead airmen..."

"But how many of those had no wounds whatsoever? That is what I am asking you."

"But you are blind! How can you be so sure?"

"Then go and see for yourself! There is not a single wound. And as a widow, am I not entitled to know what happened to my husband?"

"There's the rub, Madam. I'm sorry to have to say this, but I'm afraid your grief is leading you astray. You are grasping at straws. Just grasping at straws."

"Well, I don't understand what that has got to do with anything."

But it was useless. From the morgue, Daisy took a cab back to the RAF station and demanded to speak to the Commanding Officer. She was led to Major Mannings' office without delay. She explained the whole situation again to the major, and he listened silently, and allowed her to tell her story without interrupting. When she had finished, he remained quiet for a while, putting the fingertips of both his hands together in a mannerism that Daisy could not see, but that translated for her in an over-long silence. Finally he said, "This is a remarkable thing, Daisy, I must say. But what do you want me to do about it?"

21

"I want you to order an autopsy, so that we can ascertain exactly what caused Ralph's death."

"I'm not sure I have the authority for that. And it would seem very odd to say the least if I tried to do so. Imagine ordering an autopsy under these circumstances, when hundreds of airmen are dying every day all over Europe. It would make me the laughing stock of Bomber Command..."

"Does that matter? Is your reputation more important than my right to know?"

"No! Of course not. But there's the rub: your right to know. You see, Daisy, if I acceded to your demand it would set a very bad precedent indeed. Before long, war widows would be lining up in front of my office, clamouring for an autopsy on their deceased men. And what are you hoping to achieve anyway? I'm sorry to say that none of this is going to bring our dear Ralph back..."

"I understand that, but I feel I'm entitled to the truth about my husband's death. For all I know he could have been murdered."

"Murdered? Good God, my dear Daisy, do you really believe that my crews go about murdering one another during their bombing raids over Germany? If this kind of allegation came out, I can hardly imagine what it would do to morale. It would simply bring the war effort into jeopardy. No, no, the more I think about it, the more I feel that what you are asking of me is out of the question."

As she left the CO's office, Daisy thought, "Well, at least the major didn't reproach me for being blind." The next stop was the police station back in town. After some arguing with an old constable at the front desk, she was led to the office of the Chief Inspector. "I would like to report a crime," she said. "I have reason to believe that my husband was murdered." Having said that, she at least held the man's attention. While she was speaking, the man kept tapping on his desk with a pencil—or some such object—in a very irritating manner. Then, when Daisy had finished her story, she found to her dismay that he could hardly keep his merriment under control. His voice was wobbly with repressed laughter. "Let me get this straight: you are telling me that it is not the Germans who killed your husband, but one of our own chaps?"

"Well, I'm not accusing anyone in particular. I only want to know how my husband died. I see this as a means to an end. I want an autopsy performed on my late husband's body."

"Well, if I were you, I wouldn't be so sure that you're going to achieve that. The fact that you report a crime does not mean that a crime was actually committed. It is for me—and the coroner of course—to decide if we want to start an inquest into the matter or not. For all I know your husband could have died of a heart attack, which wouldn't be strange under the circumstances, what with flying over enemy territory and all that..."

"There was nothing wrong with Ralph's heart, and he'd already flown more than a dozen missions over Germany. He was a hardened and experienced bomber pilot. And he was far too young for heart attacks..."

"Be that as it may, I can't prevent you from filing an accusation of murder against persons unknown, but I don't have to act on it. I'm afraid your file will land in a drawer and stay there for the duration of the war. We are very busy and understaffed, what with all our younger colleagues fighting Hitler and all that. Now, you may go back to the constable at the front desk, and let him take down your deposition. He will know what to do. I take it you can find your own way with your cane? A good day to you, Madam."

As she opened the door to his office, Daisy heard the Chief Inspector grumble, still tapping away behind his desk, "Besides, if the alleged murder had been perpetrated during a bombing run, then wouldn't this be a case for the Berlin police?" And he burst out laughing, a short cackle, but he checked himself immediately when he saw that Daisy had frozen in her tracks. "Sorry!" he shouted, "not funny! blame the nerves!" As she left his office, Daisy slammed the door behind her as violently as she could.

In the train on her way back to London, Daisy felt sad, of course, and reflecting back on a strange day, she had the feeling that ages had gone by since she had been revising anatomy with her friends that morning. It seemed an eternity since the major had come knocking at her door to tell her that Ralph was dead. All this still didn't seem real.

Well, you certainly needed to bring it back to the forefront of your mind. Feeling Ralph's corpse under her fingertips had been real enough, all the features had been familiar under her touch, but so cold, so gaunt, so lifeless. Ralph had always loved it when she explored his face or his body. When they were lying in each other's arms, she liked to fondle him for what seemed to be hours on end. He would undergo her caresses quite solemnly, with utmost patience, but sometimes he couldn't help himself and he would burst out into giggles like a little boy. In the end he would seize her hand and kiss her palm or her fingertips. It had always been the most intimate thing between them.

As a child, Daisy had been taught not to touch people or their possessions. When you visited your dear old Aunt Agatha, it just wouldn't do to touch her dear old face and all the interesting knick-knacks in her parlour. Or her china. "Daisy, manners, dear." And when you burned your fingers on her hot teapot, your mother would grumble "Serves you right for always touching everything." And Mummy had never stopped to think that she was depriving her blind little girl of one of her only means of exploring the world. Thank God her parents had decided to send her to a new school for the blind, where people had much more enlightened ideas...

24

So Ralph's corpse under her fingertips had been very real indeed.

Then there had been the fact that she couldn't find any wounds, even with that nice attendant's help. That was also real. It had been quite a shock. Daisy knew all about the German flak and the night fighters and the deadly wounds inflicted by shrapnel and stray bullets. Ralph had always been brutal in his descriptions of the dangers involved in his work. He had spared her no detail. She knew from other wives and girlfriends of RAF men, that other husbands and boyfriends would avoid such subjects or gloss them over in order to spare the sensitivities of their womenfolk. With Ralph no such nonsense. At the beginning of their relationship he had said to her, "I have no idea of what a blind girl needs, so I want you to be absolutely ruthless, even brutal, in telling me about it." Then, when he had started flying on a bomber, he had applied the same principle to the discussion of his own plight.

So, when she heard that his body had been carried off the plane, Daisy had known straight away that this could mean only one thing: that Ralph had been killed by shrapnel from flak or by a stray bullet. Then, when she couldn't find any wounds, she had understood at once that this did not make any sense. The first question that came to her mind had been, "What has killed him? I need to get an autopsy done in order to ascertain what killed my dear Ralph." It was only natural. Or was she just grasping at straws as the morgue official had said?

Now, the next step had occurred in the major's office at the RAF station that second time, when she had returned to the base. All of a sudden she had been talking of murder. She had just blurted it out without thinking, and she had no idea where such a notion had come from. But was it real, though? Such ideas that just pop up in your head out of nowhere have an uncanny tendency to feel very real indeed, and completely dreamlike at the same time. For the major it had been the last straw, poor man. And in one respect he had been right: none of this was going to bring Ralph back.

But at least this notion of murder had been useful in her dealings with that very rude and stubborn Chief Inspector at the police station. Even though she hadn't been able to obtain the autopsy she wanted, filing an accusation of murder had been one step in the right direction. Her discovery at the morgue was now on record, as it were. And there was one good thing to be said about the Chief Inspector: he had demanded that she find her own way to the front desk with her cane. Nobody ever did that, but more people should. It is very nice for a blind person to be told, "You can manage on your own."

And that was exactly what she would have to do now, if she wanted any progress to be made in finding out what had happened. "I've read more Agatha Christie novels than I care to remember," Daisy reflected, "but I have never been particularly partial to the genre." On the other hand, in the Braille library at school they'd had *lots* of murder mysteries, and when you had read everything else several times over, you finally had to give in and read that low-brow stuff as well.

"So, let's see, what would you have to do as an amateur sleuth? What do we have to go on? You need to figure out the motive, the opportunity and the means. And of course alibis are always essential." With that last item at least the situation was clear: everyone who was *not* on that Lancaster during the fatal bombing run had an ironclad alibi. This seemed absurd. Daisy almost smiled: if it hadn't been so tragic, it would have been rather funny.

Now, what else was there in the toolbox? Motive. Daisy couldn't for the life of her imagine who would have wanted to kill Ralph, and for what motive that might have been. She reflected that she could go and sit on top of a mountain and think it over until she grew a long white beard, and she still wouldn't be able to come up with anything along that line. On the other hand, the Germans who were on the receiving end of all those bombs, in Berlin and elsewhere, didn't think very kindly of people like Ralph. But as Ralph himself had often argued, this was not a very useful line of reasoning when you were fighting a war. Or trying to solve a murder.

Then there was opportunity. As already mentioned, only the six men flying with Ralph on that bomber had opportunity, but they were his crew, for Pete's sake, it was out of the question that any of them should have done it. Ralph adored the crew and the crew adored him. He was the skipper. But as he had explained to her, "It is not: *my* crew, you know, we *are* the crew. Even as skipper I am just *part* of a bomber crew." They had all been together from the very beginning, when their first Lanc had been delivered to them fresh from the factory, and they had always stayed together. Daisy had often been jealous of the crew, because they were so close to Ralph, and because they went to hell and back together on a daily basis. They depended on one another for their very survival and had to be able to trust one another blindly. A bomber crew was something very special, almost like a married couple, but extended to seven men.

And then all you had left was: the means. If one of the crew had wanted to kill his skipper, he would simply have stabbed him with a knife or shot him with a pistol, as an open wound was precisely what was expected from flak shrapnel or stray bullets. No one would have noticed if Ralph had been killed with a knife or a gun. But the whole point was that there was no wound. Nothing...

Suddenly a new notion popped up in Daisy's mind: "Poison." Ralph could very well have been poisoned!

Immediately Daisy raised herself from her seat, dropping her handbag to the floor, causing quite a stir in the hushed compartment. But without even seeming to notice this, the blind girl turned around and took down her little brown suitcase from the luggage rack above her head. Then, after having picked up her handbag from the floor, she sat down with the suitcase on her lap and her handbag and cane by her side. The springs of the latches popped under her fingers. She raised the lid of the suitcase and started rummaging inside. To the other occupants of the full compartment it was a strange sight: normally, when people rummage in a suitcase on their lap, they will bend over and bow their head in order to peep intently under the lid. This girl was sitting erect, with her chin up, and focused her attention entirely on her fingertips. In a sense it seemed a very efficient way of going about a thing like that.

The suitcase was Ralph's, of course. Daisy knew it well because she had often unpacked it, with joyful anticipation, when Ralph had come home on leave, and packed it for him with a heavy heart when he was about to go back to base. That morning she had as it were been reunited with it. When Major Mannings had driven her to the RAF station, he had told her that she would be "allowed" to visit her late husband's room and that his personal affairs would be "handed over" to her. For the first time she had met Victor, Ralph's batman, though she felt she already knew him well from Ralph's stories. On this station, the batmen attended to several officers, but even so they were very close to their charges. This man's condolences had been the most heartfelt Daisy had yet received. The batman had guided her around Ralph's quarters, explaining that it was to be vacated immediately to make room for another officer, "Life can be hard that way." Then he had led her to a small pile of belongings on Ralph's bed, including the suitcase. "I believe it would be best to take away the personal affairs right now, in the suitcase. I can send on the uniforms and the other clothes by post after I've had them cleaned." He had told her that it was highly irregular for a lady to come to the officers' living quarters to pick up her husband's things in person, but that in the case of Ralph—"I mean Pilot Officer Prendergast"—you could expect anything.

The suitcase contained some toiletries, some books and notebooks, a couple of framed pictures of herself, some important-feeling papers and documents, and along with the usual personal objects—Ralph's watch, his penknife, his pocket diary—there was also a Thermos flask. Daisy had known all along that it was there. She took it out, closed the lid, and held the flask in her hands on top of the suitcase. This object too she knew well. Ralph had always taken it home with him, so that he could drink some coffee on the train, on the way home and going back. But Daisy also knew that he had taken this very same Thermos can with him on his bombing runs. Like some of the other belongings in the little brown suitcase, this flask must have been with him when he died.

Daisy lifted up the can and shook it next to her ear. By the lightness of it, it appeared to be empty, but she thought that she could hear a tiny pool of liquid slopping around at the bottom. She unscrewed the lid and held the opening to her nose. The inside clearly smelled of coffee, of course, but also rather watery. Daisy shook the open can lightly: if there was something left in it, it could not be much.

Daisy knew that there was a lady among the passengers sitting with her in the compartment. She could smell her perfume. She turned her face in the general direction where this woman was seated. "Pardon me, Madam…"

"Yes, pet?"

"Could you please take a peek at the bottom of this Thermos flask and tell me if there is anything there? Be careful not to spill it if there is…"

"Don't you worry, dear. I only have the one suit and I don't want to ruin it."

Daisy handed the Thermos flask over, and there was a long silence, while the unknown lady peeped inside it. Finally she reported, "I can see a little puddle of water with traces of coffee at the bottom of your flask. I would say that it contained coffee at first, but that it was rinsed perfunctorily just once and put away immediately without letting it drip out."

"Oh. Thank you. You're very observant, well done!"

"You're welcome, darling. I'll bet it's a man who took care of this..."

"Yes, well done again. It was my husband's batman."

"Ooh, married to a commissioned officer, are you? There's more to you than meets the eye, then..."

"I believe you could say that, yes."

As the train was slowly rumbling into London, and as Daisy had broken the ice, the other travellers in the compartment started commenting on the destruction they could see through the window, and how London had been before the war, and how were they ever going to rebuild it? Daisy reflected wistfully that she had never seen London, not before the war, not now with all the damage, and that when they would rebuild it, she would hardly know the difference.

When she finally got home to her flat in Tufnell Park that evening, Daisy felt shattered and decided to go to bed early. She wasn't hungry at all and took only a couple of digestives with a cup of tea. But even the biscuits went down with difficulty. As soon as she was lying in bed she allowed herself to weep again, this time profusely. She felt she no longer could hold the tears back; she just could not be brave anymore. It was her first night as a widow: Ralph had died above Germany only the night before. And of course, she was very much used to being alone while Ralph was away, but the knowledge that he was no longer there and would never come back made things entirely different and was hard to take.

The next morning she woke up early, and felt a burning and throbbing sensation around her eyelids. She knew what that meant, even though it hadn't happened for many years: an inflammation of her atrophied tear-ducts.

She had a quick breakfast and went out. She took the Thermos flask with her in a shoulder bag, a somewhat larger one than her usual handbag. Then she went straight to the local chemist's a few streets from her block of flats. Mr Dobbs was alone at this early hour, as Daisy had hoped. As he asked her what he could do for her, Daisy took off her dark glasses and showed him her eyes. "The first thing, Mister Dobbs, is that I believe I'm having an inflammation of the tear-ducts. Would you have something to soothe that?"

"Yes, of course, Mrs Prendergast. I'll give you an antiseptic salve, but I would recommend that you show that to your GP as well..."

Then Daisy took the Thermos flask out of her bag and asked him if he would be able to do a chemical analysis of the contents, even though there were only a few drops left, and that they were quite diluted at that. The pharmacist asked, "Can you tell me what you have in mind? I can certainly try to do an analysis, but it would help if I knew what I'm looking for."

"Well, I was thinking along the lines of poison, like rat poison, cyanide or strychnine. You know, the kind of thing that a murderer in an Agatha Christie novel would use to poison someone..."

"Good Lord! My dear Mrs Prendergast, are you serious? Shouldn't you go straight to the police with this kind of inquiry?"

Daisy explained that she had already done precisely that, and told the friendly old pharmacist her story. After having heard her out, Mr Dobbs said, "Very well my poor Mrs Prendergast, I understand the urgency now. I will give it my best... Come back at the beginning of the afternoon for the results. Oh, and may I convey my most sincere and heartfelt condolences for your loss? Erm... does the tear-duct inflammation have something to do with that by any chance?"

"I'm afraid so, yes. That is one of the biggest burdens of my birth defect, you know: I cannot weep without suffering great discomforts afterwards..."

When Daisy came back in the afternoon, the pharmacist's shop was quite busy with customers, but Mrs Dobbs was helping her husband and the pharmacist could free himself for the blind young woman. He led her to the back of the shop and expostulated excitedly, "Mrs Prendergast, you have been vindicated! I have found traces of arsenic in the sample! Yes, that's right: arsenic. Now, it is impossible to say if the coffee contained a lethal dose, as we have no idea how much it was watered down, but the simple fact that some arsenic was there allows us to assume that the coffee was laced with poison."

"This is incredible! How clever of you, Sir! Could you put what you just said to me in writing? You know, in an official way, in your capacity as a registered pharmacist?"

"Of course, Madam. I see what you mean."

"And could you make a duplicate? I need to send a copy to that very rude and stubborn Chief Inspector..."

"Yes, yes, I'll even do one better: with two sheets of carbon paper, I can type it out in triplicate. And I'll drop it in your mailbox as soon as I'm done, first thing after closing time."

"Mister Dobbs, you're an angel," Daisy said, and she leaned over and gave him a kiss that grazed his grizzled cheek.

When she left the pharmacy, Daisy put her hand on the Thermos can inside her shoulder bag, and while she probed her way back home with the white cane in her other hand, she reflected, "I am now positive that Ralph was actually murdered. I know this for a fact and I'm holding the murder weapon right here in my hand."

II   1939: How Daisy met Ralph

Going places can be a bit daunting. There's a reason why some people always spend their summer holidays at the same family pension in Brighton, booking early to make sure they'll have the very same rooms as they had the year before.

For the blind, of course, the unknown is even more daunting than for normal people. Each time they go to a new place, they enter a netherworld and have to navigate the mists of a new territory on trust alone. But at sixteen, going on seventeen, Daisy was only too eager to take on such challenges.

As she and her mother stood waiting at the front door of Bottomleigh House, the monumental portico with its classical columns filled the older woman with awe and foreboding. For the young girl, who was not even aware of the splendour of the place, it was the twinkle of the old-fashioned bell that made her heart leap with anticipation.

"I don't understand why you can't come with us to Brighton this year, as usual. What was Daddy thinking!"

"Maybe: that you two are going to have a wonderful time without me. I'm sure he was just thinking of having a second honeymoon!"

"Oh hush, Daisy... such rot! You don't even know what you're talking about!"

"Hush, Mummy, I'm a big girl now... I wouldn't mind a little bit of romance of my own, provided I can find Mister Right."

This was said very airily, but Daisy felt far less self-assured than she wanted her mother to believe. Boys were a great mystery to her, the object of much speculation, fantasising and soul-searching. At school she and the other blind girls discussed the topic endlessly, and the consensus was that one was better off without Boys. If only you could stay at school forever, spend your whole life living exclusively with other blind girls... But still.

Presently the door opened, and Daisy and her mother were ushered into the entrance hall by a footman of some sort. Daisy could hear their footfalls and the tapping of her cane echoing through what must have been a wide and high hall. Breathing in deeply, she could smell the musty odour of antiques typical of such a place. Then their hosts stepped forward and introduced themselves as "Mr and Mrs Prendergast". This charmingly mild-mannered couple led their two guests to what they referred to as the "family living room" and immediately proceeded to "call the children." Shortly a noisy gang of young people invaded the room. They were about Daisy's age by the sound of it, and were first introduced collectively as "the gang". Too many names and too many handshakes followed at too fast a clip: William, Cedric, Margaret, Joan. They were not siblings but more or less cousins. Daisy didn't say a word, but felt to her great despair that she was blushing to the roots of her hair.

Then there was one Beatrice, who stepped forward and kissed her on the cheek, which pleased Daisy immensely. At her school she and her best friends were hugging all the time: you knew one another by touch, and particularly by smell. It's like when you visit other people's homes: you'll notice without even trying that each house has its own distinctive smell. Beatrice smelled very nice indeed. And then Ralph was called forward by his father, who introduced him especially as her host, as he was the eldest son of the house, "If you need anything, you must ask Ralph."

"Welcome to the madhouse," Ralph said pleasantly, shaking her hand.

Daisy didn't reply, as she didn't know what to say. She only smiled, unwittingly unleashing the full power of seduction of her pearly teeth and lovely dimples.

Tea was served, accompanied by lively conversation from all quarters; Daisy did not participate much, speaking only briefly when spoken to, just like her mother. The young people were talking without a pause, mainly among themselves, with a mixture of absurd humour and aggressive teasing that relied on a lot of innuendo to deliver its punches. It was going to take some doing to get this lively "gang" figured out, but Daisy, sitting silently in the middle of the hubbub, was already working on it.

After tea she was shown to her room, accompanied by her mother. Very thoughtfully her hostess had given her a room right at the top of the first flight of stairs, "I hope that will make it easier for you to find your way around the house." Left alone with her mother, Daisy made a quick assessment of her room, touching everything, which still made her mother edgy, though by now she knew better than to remonstrate. She helped her daughter unpack her suitcase and put away her things. Then it was time to say goodbye, as she was to leave her on her own at Bottomleigh House. Mrs Hayes choked up and became a bit tearful. "Don't worry, Mummy," Daisy said. "I'll be fine, these are nice people, I intend to have a good time."

She had been invited by the Prendergast family to spend two weeks here at Bottomleigh House, and for her it was a first, a leap into an unknown world. Her own family were not gentry at all. Her father was a bank manager, who happened to have done a very good job at managing Mr Prendergast's finances in difficult times. But as Daddy always said, "All it needs is to focus on the assets, only the assets." Daisy had no idea what that meant, but anyway, this had led the master of Bottomleigh House to become aware of Daisy's existence. He had been quite charmed when he had met her for the first time, and forthwith he had issued an invitation.

And now, as soon as she had finished waving goodbye to her mother at the front door and the taxi had disappeared at the end of the drive, Ralph appeared at her side and offered to show her around the house. "Oh yes," Daisy said, "that would be very useful, thank you." The other young people were no longer there. They were nowhere to be heard.

"I must say, Ralph, you're being an impeccable host. But then of course those are your father's orders..."

"Well, Daddy has the wisdom never to give me orders that I wouldn't obey with great pleasure. That is, during the summer hols, at least."

"Aha... So: now I must ask you to take my hand and hold me close to you, I'm afraid that's the way it's done with a blind person."

"Very well," Ralph replied, and they proceeded to explore the ground floor room by room, hand in hand. This of course was the part of the house where the guests were expected to move around freely; all the bedrooms upstairs Daisy didn't need to know. In each new chamber, Daisy insisted on being led around the four walls, then wanted to go criss-cross all over the place. While exploring like this she asked where the windows were and where the doors; what pieces of furniture were there. She mapped each new space in her mind, and its position with respect to the rest of the house. Ralph would have found this task excruciatingly tedious, if it had not been for the novelty of getting to know a blind girl, and a very pretty one at that. It took a couple of hours. From then on

Daisy knew as well how Ralph smelled. Now she had been properly introduced to Beatrice and him. Four to go.

After that, dinner and the evening were pleasant and uneventful. At the dinner table the young people were on their best behaviour, and Daisy was introduced to half a dozen grown-up guests; there were also younger children, who in this house were allowed to dine with the adults. Among the grown-ups was Ralph's elder sister, Maud, and among the children his little sister, Margery.

The table conversations were dominated by the adults, but not entirely devoid of interest. Ralph's parents were very political, Labourites of long standing; they invited people from all walks of life to the manor for summer parties where social utopias were dreamed up and discussed endlessly. When you heard such ideas debated for the very first time, as was the case for Daisy, it was actually rather thrilling.

The evening was spent mostly listening to a play on the wireless, a murder mystery, which Daisy found very agreeable as it allowed her to relax without having to make an effort at conversation. And that was precisely why her hostess, Mrs Prendergast, had chosen this form of entertainment on this occasion.

There had been one awkwardness, however, but Daisy was not aware of it. Her mother had prepared an evening dress for her and instructed her to wear it at dinner without fail. "Put this on as soon as you hear the gong..." But at Bottomleigh, one did not change for dinner, at least not in the summer, and Daisy's attire had been a bit jarring. She was overdressed, but showing too much of her shoulders and bosom, which had attracted a great deal of attention, from male and female fellow-dinner-guests alike. No one had said a word about it, of course, and Daisy had remained blissfully unaware of her *faux pas*.

The next morning Daisy had no trouble finding her way

to the breakfast room, with a little help from her cane. But when she entered the room, she found it very quiet and wondered if she had overslept, even though the alarm on her tactile travel clock had gone off at the appointed hour. Then her hostess cried, "Daisy! I was waiting for you. Good morning, dear. Did you sleep well? Come and sit by my side."

"Am I late, Mrs Prendergast?"

"No, no, not at all, let me serve you something. What do you want?"

"Where is everybody? I mean, where are the others?"

"I'm afraid they've already left. They seem to have left very early today. You know: eager to go on the adventure of the day... I'm dreadfully sorry about their lack of consideration for you as a guest. I will certainly remonstrate with them..."

"Oh no, please, Mrs Prendergast, that would not be helpful at all. I'm sure we'll get along just fine if we give it some time..."

"Well, that's awfully gracious of you, my dear Daisy. In the meantime I'm sure we can find something interesting for you to do today. Do you ride horses? Or would you like to learn? We have excellent stables, we can find a suitably compliant mount for you, and surely riding is something a blind person can do with great pleasure..."

"Well thank you, Mrs Prendergast; it's very kind of you to offer, but no. I've tried riding at school and I didn't like it much, I'm afraid. I find horses, and even ponies, rather unwieldy and I don't like the way they smell."

"Well, in these parts that's a most unusual point of view, I must say..."

Mrs Prendergast was a bit annoyed and wondering what else she could offer this rather peculiar girl, when her son appeared at the breakfast table. "Ralph!" she cried, "are you still there? Didn't you leave with your gang this morning? What on earth is going on!"

Ralph kissed his mother and greeted Daisy with a big smile, which she of course could not see. "I gave them the slip this morning. Serves them right. Last night they kept banging on about the fact that they didn't want Daisy to join us on our daily outing and that having her along would cramp our style and spoil all the fun. So they decided to go bicycling, because you can't be expected to take a blind guest along on a bicycling trip. I hope you won't take this too personally, Daisy..."

"Oh no, Ralph, I quite understand. I was just saying to your mother: we must give it some time."

"Exactly! So I decided to give them the slip and spend my day with you. I must entertain our charming new guest!"

His mother remarked that Daisy and she were just discussing the subject of entertainment, but that poor Daisy didn't care much for riding. "Well, Daisy," said Ralph, "maybe you yourself have a better idea? What is it that you'd like to do today?"

The young girl cocked her head as if she were looking sideways at the boy who was taking a seat next to her at the table. But in fact she was directing her ear straight at him and trying to gauge his expression, his mood, by hearing. "What I really would like to do today is to learn to ride a bicycle."

"You mean like riding along on a tandem?"

"Oh no, I don't suppose you have one of those anyway. I mean a normal bicycle. Do you think you could teach me?"

The young man sitting next to her gasped, then reflected for a few seconds, and said slowly, "Well... yes, why not, I guess I could do that, but it might take a little longer than one day."

"Then let's do it!" the girl exclaimed. "Let's start straight after breakfast!"

Ralph took Daisy to the metalled courtyard in front of

the garages, retrieved a smallish women's bike that had belonged to Maud when she was thirteen or fourteen years old, and some tools. He then proceeded to unscrew the pedals, and he bound the pedal crank to the frame of the bike with a piece of string. Next he lowered the saddle and secured it in such a position that the girl could easily stand on her feet while straddling the saddle. All the while Daisy crouched next to him and explored the bicycle with both hands, going over the tubes of the frame, feeling the tyres and poking at the spokes. In the end her fingertips were a bit greasy and Ralph offered a clean rag.

By then he had completed the adjustments. "*Et voilà*, a nice draisine for you, a dandy horse, so that you can learn to ride with both feet on the ground."

"My dear Ralph, you're a real genius at mechanics!" Daisy cried.

"So you know the difference between a draisine and a bicycle?"

"Of course! I may be blind, but I'm not retarded!"

Ralph thought, "Ooh, the girl can be prickly!"

"No, but seriously," he persisted, "just out of curiosity. How do you happen to know such things?"

"Same as you, I guess. I read about it in the ency-clopedia. We have a Braille encyclopedia at school and I read that from A to Z. And I have an excellent memory, so I know everything this particular encyclopedia has to tell about the world."

"Well I must say, you seem to be something of a genius yourself!"

"No! That's my point: apart from being blind, I'm just an ordinary person. I read books and magazines—in Braille—, I listen to the wireless, and I know what's going on in the world because I'm interested in things. Just like you. Besides, have you ever seen a *real* dandy horse yourself?"

"As a matter of fact, I have. At the Science Museum!

"Oh! Right. Lucky you."

"But I get your point, Daisy. I was just being a bit nosy, sorry."

"Oh, but don't apologize, please! Feel free to ask anything you want. Now what do we do with this dandy horse?"

Ralph thought it over for a second. "Actually, the first thing I want you to do is to take off your glasses and hand them over to me for safe-keeping. I'm afraid you might fall and break them and cut yourself."

Without a word, Daisy took off her glasses and revealed the empty buttonholes of her crippled eyes in their full horror. Ralph was taken aback and fascinated at the same time. He started counting to ten in his mind while still peering intently at the ghoulish slits. Even the eyelids were atrophied; there were no eyelashes. After counting to ten, Ralph told himself, "All right, I'm over it now." Then he reflected that the sight of Daisy's eyes was disturbing and thrilling at the same time. She looked so naked. It was almost as if she'd taken off her clothes for him. There was something uncannily intimate about this situation.

"Is everything all right?" Daisy asked.

"Yes, yes. I just had to swallow hard, that's all."

"Funny, I didn't hear anything."

"No, I meant: swallow hard mentally."

"Oh! Good. So what do I do now?"

Ralph made Daisy sit on the saddle and put her hands on the handlebars, and then her fingers on the brake levers; then he explained how it all was supposed to work. "Now I just want you to step forwards and try to steer left and right and test those brakes. There's enough room in this courtyard, and I'll give a shout when you must come back." And so the lessons began.

By the time they heard the gong and had to stop to go

41

inside for lunch, Daisy was already able to coast nicely after giving a few swift kicks on the ground with her feet, then letting both legs dangle left and right. She was getting the hang of it and feeling quite exhilarated by the progress she had made. But to achieve this, she'd had to work relentlessly. She had kept at it for several hours now, and Ralph's voice had become hoarse from guiding her movements. Standing in a central spot of the garage courtyard, he had kept shouting instructions, "A little to the left, you're almost there. Brake! Brake! Turn around and come back to me..." It had required his utmost concentration and he felt exhaustted. On the way to the kitchen entrance of the house, holding her hand and handing back her glasses, he told Daisy, "I'm amazed at how well you are doing. I expected you would have much more trouble with your sense of balance."

"Oh no, there's nothing wrong with my cochlea. People tend to overestimate the role their eyesight plays in keeping their balance. At school they told us that, in fact, the inner ear takes over completely, the moment normal people stop looking at their own feet!"

At the lunch table there was still no sign of the gang. Ralph's father, having been told by his wife what was going on, appeared to be quite angry about it. "I wager that Cookie is the instigator of this caper, as usual! Ralph?"

"I am not at liberty to tell, Sir."

"You don't need to. I know enough! The presence of that girl spells trouble each and every time..."

"Well, I beg you not to be too harsh on Cookie this time, father. The truth of the matter is that we had a lover's tiff, Cookie and I, if *lover* is the correct word in this case. Yesterday we had a falling out that led us to end our relationship, if a *relationship* is really what we had... Anyway, this morning Cookie was in a murderous mood so I gladly let her go with the whole gang. I gave them my blessing."

"So *you* are responsible, then. Bad show of hospitality towards our charming new guest!"

"Oh, but I have been making amends to Daisy... I have been teaching her to ride a bicycle!"

"I beg your pardon? My poor Daisy, what has this young blackguard been subjecting you to? Are you certain you can do this? It seems a bit dangerous for a blind person, if I may say so."

"Well, don't blame Ralph, Sir. It was entirely my idea. I see it as an interesting challenge. I would like to go bicycling in the countryside with the others, just tagging along on the open road, navigating by the sounds the others make. It should be feasible..."

"You make it sound quite easy, but have you ever done this kind of thing before?"

"Bicycling, no. But navigating by sound, *that* we blind people do all the time. The thing is, when we go tap-tapping with our white cane, we're not only probing our way, but also listening to the reflections of the sound we produce... It's called 'echolocation'. That's why I believe that bicycling should be quite feasible for me."

"Very well. But be careful you two, I beg of you."

When they went back to the courtyard in front of the garages after lunch, hand in hand, Daisy asked Ralph, "Who is Cookie? Do I know her?"

"Yes, that's what we always call Margaret. I have no idea why we call her that..."

"I hope your falling out had nothing to do with me..."

"Oh no! Don't worry, it had been brewing for a long time. You just happened to arrive at a very bad moment, that's all. But I'm sure everything is going to be all right and that we're all going to be good friends in the end."

Now Ralph untied the crank and fastened the pedals back on his sister's bicycle. The saddle was repositioned just a little bit higher, and Daisy was to pedal in earnest for the first time. With Ralph holding the saddle and running next to her, she managed a wobbly start. Then Ralph let go of the saddle for a very short while, and then a little longer, and suddenly Daisy was off. It was exactly how little Margery had done it only a few years before. Then Daisy almost crashed into a garage door and Ralph was shouting "Brake! Brake! Feet on the ground!" Daisy stopped just in time, then toppled over with her machine, but she didn't hurt herself.

By the end of the afternoon, after she had again kept at it relentlessly, Daisy could ride a bicycle. As she was rather tall, Ralph had soon decided to abandon Maud's old machine and had fetched a full-size model that was kept at the disposal of grown-up female guests. His pupil fitted the bill exactly. Then, as soon as she had become used to that one, he brought out his own bike, went to the house to get a deck of playing cards, fixed a card to his frame in such a way that it flapped against the spokes of his rear wheel, and tested that it made a good sound.

Daisy said, "Another stroke of genius! You're a real boffin."

"It's funny that you should say that. Normally William is our great boffin, but in his absence I suppose I'll have to play the understudy."

And now that everything was ready, Ralph said to Daisy, "Follow me, keep right behind me, we're going for a proper ride."

The card produced an astonishingly loud rattling noise and Ralph started riding down the driveway that led from the front of Bottomleigh House to the main road, all the while casting glances behind him to make sure that Daisy kept up with him. It went astonishingly well and they picked up some speed. Suddenly Daisy started to shout with girlish excitement, "Ralph! Ralph! I'm actually riding a bicycle! I'm free! I'm flying! Yahoo!"

Relentlessly they spent the next hour riding up and down the driveway, a distance of about five hundred yards. Then, at a given moment, the gang turned up at the main gate, finally back from their day-long trip in the countryside. They were quite astounded at the sight of the blind girl chasing after Ralph at breakneck speed on her bicycle, shouting "Tally-ho!" at the top of her lungs, and they felt at once that it was they, not them, who had missed all the fun that day.

Before they finally went back into the house to prepare for dinner, after the gong had sounded, Ralph took Daisy aside and told her, "Today there's no need to change, Daisy, just keep to the kind of thing you're wearing now, we're having an informal evening."

"Oh dear, did I make a fool of myself last night?"

"No! No. On the contrary, you looked very fetching, you made a great impression."

"You're astoundingly bad at lying, Ralph. I like that about you."

That night, as Daisy was preparing to go to bed, there was a knocking at her door. She just had time to put her dark glasses back on before the door opened and a girl's voice inquired, "Can we come in? Are you decent and all that?"

"Yes, yes, do come in," she replied. Then she heard the rustle of several people pouring into her room.

"Booh, it's dark in here!" one of the boys said. "Were you already asleep?"

"No, but I'm blind, remember? I don't need any light."

The switch by the door produced its characteristic click.

"We would like to ask you something." the first girl's voice said.

"Who is this, by the way?"

"It's me, Cookie, well, Margaret, and the rest of the gang."

"Ah yes, Cookie! I was wondering: why does everyone call you that?"

"Well, you see, my mother's an American. And when I was a little girl, wherever we went visiting, I always asked for cookies. 'I want a cookie', I would cry. I must admit that I had deplorable manners at the time."

"Oh, but you still have," the others laughed, "you still have!"

"All right," Daisy said, "what can I do for you and the rest of the gang? I believe Ralph is not with you? Beatrice?"

"No," Beatrice replied. "Ralph is exhausted, truly exhausted. He went to bed early. What on earth did you do to him?"

"I'm afraid I drove him rather hard today, poor boy. Though it was worth it: I learned to bicycle! But anyway, what did you want to ask?"

"Well," Cookie said, "the thing is, we'd like to see your eyes..."

"Oh, so Ralph has told you about that... before he went to bed."

"No, no. The thing is, we saw you from a distance when you were bicycling. You weren't wearing your dark glasses."

"Never mind. It's all the same to me, you know. You can see my eyes if that's what you want, but on one condition..."

"Oh, good," one of the boys said. "You're driving up the suspense..."

"Yes... I want us all to have a nice old-fashioned pillow fight afterwards."

"A pillow fight?" Cookie exclaimed. "Aren't we a bit old for such a childish thing?"

"Well, you're childish enough to ask a blind girl to show you her crippled eyes, so why on earth not? Besides, I'm proposing a very special kind of pillow fight. One we always organize at school when a new girl joins us. Now you run back to your rooms and fetch your pillows. Then I'll show

46

you what you want to see..."

In a moment the gang were back with their pillows, and Daisy told them to close the door and motioned them to come and sit by her side on the bed. Then she slowly took of her glasses and put them away.

"Ugh!"

"Disgusting!"

"The horror!" they all cried, and Daisy started giggling, because such a frank reaction was most unusual and rather unexpected. Beatrice leaned over and spoke softly in her ear, "You don't mind, really?"

"No, really, it's quite all right. Tomorrow I'll go bicycling with all of you and I won't be wearing my glasses, so we might as well get it over with now."

And then, when they were all done making a show of how horrible they found her eyes, Cookie said, "Now, for that pillow fight of yours, what's the deal?"

"Well, there are two rules. First, everyone has to keep repeating their name, like Daisy... Daisy... Daisy... so that blind people can identify you and know your position. Then secondly, you're not allowed to throw your pillow, only to hit the other players at close quarters. Now let's get going!"

And the game started. At once a mishmash of repeated names was heard: Beatrice... William... Joan... Cedric... Daisy... Cookie... and everyone started hitting everyone else over the head with their pillow. Soon the young people were drawn into the spirit of the thing and the battle became quite fierce. Daisy made sure to engage each member of the group in close combat, one after the other, and by doing so she was able to individualise the sound of each voice and find out how each one of them smelled. Then they all ended up in a heap on the Persian rug in the middle of the room, helpless with laughter, and Cookie exclaimed, "This is impossible! When you keep repeating your own name it becomes complete gibberish..."

"Yes," Daisy panted, "that's why we do it. Isn't it fun? This is how we welcome new girls at my school."

The next morning they all got up early and went bicycling straight after breakfast. It worked quite nicely. At first Ralph used his rattling playing card but the others found that too noisy. Daisy assured them she would be quite all right just tagging along, following the rustle of their machines, and of course the sound of their voices. Then Ralph decided that as driving off the side of the road was the biggest danger, Daisy should be flanked at all times by two people riding alongside her, left and right, "just like a fighter wing in the RAF." That is what they did and indeed it worked well. When a car overtook them or an oncoming one passed them, which didn't occur often on these country lanes, the wingmen or wing-girls would close in on the blind girl to protect her. The normal bends in the road were no problem, only when a sharp turn had to be made, for instance to take a side-way at a crossing, they would have to stop and Daisy would manoeuvre her bicycle by hand.

And so the gang rode on, quite at ease, joking and laughing and calling over to one another. They commented on the dressing-down Ralph's father had given Cookie at dinner last night. "Oh the humiliation!" she cried. "Everybody is always blaming *me* at Bottom-of-my-backside House!"

They all laughed at that.

"Anyway, Ralph, you're finished," William said. "Cookie hates you now."

"That wouldn't be the first time," Ralph quietly replied. "I'll survive yet again."

"By the way, Cookie has already found a new love interest," Joan announced. "Haven't you, Cookie?"

"What are you talking about, you rambling old maid?"

"I'm simply referring to the fact that Cedric did not leave

your side for one minute all day, yesterday, and that you seemed quite amenable..."

"Well, he was just being his usual pain in the bottom of the backside, and as for *amenable*, that's only your imagination."

"Thank you very much for that, Lady Cookie-cutter!" Cedric interjected, "I was only trying to cheer you up."

"And did I promise you everlasting love in exchange? No. So back off!"

William remarked, "You know, Cookie, I prefer having Cedric pining for you all day long, rather than shooting pigs!"

Everybody burst out laughing. Then they had to explain the thing to Daisy. "Our friend here once shot a pig with a dumdum bullet," William exclaimed excitedly. "Is that crazy or is that crazy?"

"The pig died instantly, just one bullet and its head exploded!"

"Ralph's dad was furious! The pig belonged to one of his tenants."

"Cedric was grounded for a week, the local equivalent of capital punishment!"

The culprit laughed sheepishly. "Please don't hold this against me, Daisy. It was only a phase. I was fascinated by heavy ammunition and managed to get hold of a couple of dumdum bullets. So the temptation to experiment a bit became too much for me... I was just a child!"

"What are you talking about?" Ralph sniggered. "It was only last summer!"

"So what? That's a long time ago! Now let's change the subject, shall we?"

After a lull in the conversation, Joan said, "What I find wonderful to witness, Ralph, is how sweet Daisy here has you completely in her clutches..."

"Yes, yes," the others concurred. "There's no escaping Daisy's pretty little clutches!"

"Gentle Daisy is indeed driving you rather hard, Ralph," Beatrice remarked. "Last night you were exhausted."

Daisy blushed, but felt compelled to intervene. "That's because poor Ralph is such a gentleman. I must confess I have exploited his goodwill shamelessly. Blind people will do that to you. We tend to lean too heavily on the brave souls who are willing to help us. So beware, Ralph!"

"That's all right, Daisy. No harm done, really."

"Speaking of which: the fact that I only fell once, and *after* I had braked, is a great tribute to your dedication..."

For lunch the gang settled in a field at the top of a hill to eat their sandwiches. The lively conversation was picked up where they had left it a moment before on the road. "How does it feel to be blind, by the way," Cedric asked Daisy. "Do you suffer a lot in silence and maintain a stiff upper lip, and all that?"

"No, not at all. I was born like this and you don't really miss what you've never had. Besides, there are advantages. You could be as ugly as a scarecrow and it wouldn't make any difference to me, and then I could very well fall in love with you, based entirely on your sparkling personality..."

"Oh but Cedric *is* a scarecrow!" they all cried. "A real horror! Quasimodo!"

"No he is not," Daisy admonished. "You can't fool me. I happen to know that Cedric is quite good-looking. Almost as good-looking as Ralph, I would say..."

"But how can you tell?" they all wanted to know.

"Well, as you normal people are all so obsessed with how you look, you give away a lot of information about it all the time. Just by listening to the interactions in the group here, I mean the way you talk to each other, I can determine quite clearly who is good-looking and who is not."

"Interesting," Cookie said. "So tell us what you've found out. How do *I* look, for instance?"

"Well, Cookie, I would say that the one with the biggest

mouth must be the prettiest to look at. But that is putting it very crudely, of course... No, the thing is, beneath all the bluster, you always seem to receive the deference that is owed to the good-looking, even from Ralph's father. And then there's the typical self-regard of the beautiful that is implicitly present in every word you utter."

"Fine, but the deference and the self-regard could be entirely due to my superior intellect!"

"Well, you *are* very intelligent and spirited as well, I won't deny it..."

"I'm a lot smarter than the rest of this lot, that's for sure!"

"... But that has nothing to do with it. I can plainly hear how attractive you must be. I can contrast this with Beatrice's case. She's just as smart as you are, but none of you ever pays much attention to anything she says, and she seems to assume that this is as it should be, so she accepts that she is not very attractive to others. And probably she isn't... Not that it makes any difference to me, Beatrice, as I said."

"What about me?" Joan piped up. "Would you say that *I* am good looking? Or not?"

"Joan? I find you hard to make out. You're such a good gossip, if I may say so, that everyone finds everything you say quite fascinating. But it tells me nothing about your appearance..."

"And what about you, Daisy?" Beatrice asked. "Does this superhuman awareness apply to yourself? Have you any idea whether you are attractive or not?"

"There's nothing superhuman about it, I just focus on what I hear. And yes, I can apply that to myself as well. So, apart from everything else, what with being blind and rather off-putting, I do believe that I am attractive. It's always 'our charming guest,' and 'sweet gentle Daisy' and whatnot. But more interesting is the part that is *not* being spoken out openly. I have reason to believe that I am very sexy..."

"Sexy!" They all cried. "Well-well, now it's getting interesting!"

"Yes, I must be quite sexy. When men—and boys—see me for the first time, they tend to gasp and make gulping sounds, and they pant ever so slightly without even realising it. I believe I can cause quite a stir. I guess I must have a rather fetching figure..."

"Especially when you are wearing that lovely little black dress," William remarked. "Like on the first evening, at dinner..."

"Oh yes, a dreadful blunder! I was so nervous I didn't even notice. So much for superhuman awareness!"

"If I had known that you would be wearing an evening dress," Cedric commented amiably, "I would have been delighted to put on my white tie. I find all the affected informality at Bottomleigh House rather tedious. When you happen to be the Earl of Haverford, why pretend you're a nobody? I'd rather have the old man behaving in a more dignified way, and that the servants know their place."

"Hush, Cedric," Ralph said. "We all know that you're a pompous old fogey at heart!"

"Well anyway," Daisy said, "formal or informal, all that is rather theoretical. Appearances mean nothing to me. I have no way of visualising any of this in my mind. And also, it's ironic when you stop to think about it: what's the good of having eyes, if it's only to become the slave of how you look to others?"

"Great," Cookie grumbled. "Now we're supposed to feel humbled, huh?"

"Well, why on earth not?"

At the end of the afternoon, when they drove home, Daisy felt quite exhausted. She suddenly realised that the tables had been turned on her. Today, for hours on end, she had been the one who had to summon the utmost concentration required to stay on course and not to crash into anyone. But then again, it had been worth it.

For the next few days the gang went out bicycling again, and once they were even able to ride as far as the seashore.

Then one morning Cedric told them that his dad would be coming to visit in the afternoon.

"Uncle Clifton!" they all cried, and explained to Daisy what this meant and why it was such exciting news. Cedric's father had been a fighter pilot in the Great War, "not really a well-known Ace, but still..." He was now a bigwig in the RAF, and when he needed to go somewhere, anywhere, he flew there in his Tiger Moth, just like other people would use their car for their daily trips. So when he came, he would be landing on the big lawn in front of Bottomleigh House. They were going to wait for him, it was out of the question to go bicycling that day, and Daisy felt some relief at that...

After a long wait in the muggy afternoon, they finally heard a buzzing sound, then Cedric cried "There! I can see it!" and the sound grew louder as the aircraft approached. At length it arrived and circled the grounds a few times, giving everyone ample opportunity to wave, jump, shout, and make complete fools of themselves. Then at last Cedric's dad landed on the lawn with noisy coughs and bangs from his backfiring engine. Later that afternoon they were all taken up for a short flight in the two-seater, even the girls; even Daisy. With Cedric and Ralph standing on the walkways of the wings and William pushing from behind, they hoisted her into the passenger seat of the Tiger Moth, and Uncle Clifton took her up for a spin in the sky. Again Daisy shouted "Yahoo! I'm flying! I'm free!" but because of the leather flight helmet and the din of the engine, the "uncle" sitting behind her at the controls didn't even hear it.

The next day it became clear that the weather was

taking a turn for the worse and that they would have to stay home a while longer because of the rain. At the breakfast table that morning, everyone discussed the plans for the day forlornly and animatedly. That is, the discussion was animated, but the plans seemed rather forlorn. Play cards? Stage a play? Read?

Ralph asked Daisy, "Do you have Braille playing cards?"

"They exist, of course, but I don't happen to have a deck with me. As for the play, that sounds lovely, but in order for me to participate, it would be better if I had the script in Braille. Though I guess one could manage without..."

Suddenly Cedric exclaimed, "I know what we could do today!"

"Yes, yes, we know," the others cried. "The shooting range!"

"No but seriously, I just had a brilliant idea! It's about Daisy... Daisy, would you like to learn to shoot?"

Before Daisy could even start to say anything, the others were crying, "That's absurd! How could such a thing even be possible!"

Daisy giggled, "Now I *am* really curious! Let Cedric tell us his idea. How do you want to go about it, Cedric?"

"Well it's quite simple, really. We mount a brass bell to the target, with a string attached, so that we can ring the bell from the shooting stand, and you aim at the sound and shoot!"

"Yes, it might work. I'd like to try that, why not? Let's do it! Let's start straight after breakfast!"

Sarcastically Cookie inquired, "But don't they have a shooting range at your school, Daisy? I would have expected that you'd have already become a crack shot, a sharpshooter even, at that school of yours..."

Daisy just ignored her.

In a barn on a disused farmyard, at the limit of the park

surrounding Bottomleigh House, there was a shooting range with rudimentary facilities. On rainy days one could practice there under shelter. After breakfast, the whole gang repaired to the place with pistols, ammunition, earmuffs, target cards, and a brass bell of the kind used at dinner to summon the next dish. Not everyone was as passionate as Cedric about shooting, but they all wanted to witness Daisy's first steps in this new endeavour.

The bell was mounted on top of a target card on the wooden panels that covered a thick wall at the back of the barn. A length of string was led to the shooting tables at the front. Then practice could begin. Cedric positioned himself behind Daisy, his arms around her left and right, his hands on her wrists, and helped her with firing the first shots. "You have to get the recoil under control before we can go on," he shouted to her through the earmuffs.

"What a romantic picture, what a platonic embrace," Joan remarked.

"Oh! act your age," Ralph remonstrated, "if only in make-believe."

But Daisy didn't mind Cedric's physical closeness, she was a lot more tolerant of this kind of thing than most people would normally be. After a while she was ready to fire a shot on her own. She took off the muffs, pulled at the string and listened carefully, slowly shaking her head from left to right and back. Then she picked up the pistol and aimed. "Ring the bell once more, Cedric."

Before the brass stopped resonating, Daisy fired her first shot, smack into the card, albeit not in the centre of it. Everyone applauded. It was a remarkable result. They egged her on to shoot some more. And then the girls, who were otherwise not particularly adept at this, wanted to try their hand as well, to see if they could better a blind girl. It was great fun.

But when they all went back to the house for lunch,

once they were sitting at the table, Daisy said, "You know, Cedric, this was very exciting, and you are a good teacher. So thank you very much for that. However, I don't think I should go on with it. You see, I'm a bit afraid it might damage my hearing, and that would be very bad indeed..."

"That's all right," Cedric answered meekly. "If you had become any better at this, you would have started destroying one brass bell after the other."

"Well, at least now, if we decide to put on a play, I could be a very convincing villain and fire a pistol at all and sundry!"

And that is what they did. That afternoon they started putting on a play, or rather a sketch, that they invented themselves as they went along. It was an absurd spoof on murder mysteries, where the corpse (Daisy) turned out to be the villain, and everybody ended up dead, piled in a heap in the middle of the rug that served as a stage. Then they decided to hash it out some more, and tinker at their new play until they could perform it in front of the whole house party. So the project kept them very busy for another rainy day.

The whole gang participated in equal measure, it was really a joint effort. Only William did not take part in it at all. He was not there. The others explained to Daisy, "William's on a mission. That sometimes happens. He is our boffin, our inventor. He locks himself up in his room and cooks up some new device. Let's just wait and see what he comes up with this time. It's always very entertaining."

That evening, just after dinner, the new sketch was performed in front of the whole family and their guests, including the children, and all the members of the staff. They had been summoned to the drawing room, where Joan and Cookie stood by the door and shouted, "Come inside, come inside! Welcome to the show!"

The girls were looking unwittingly sexy, with heavy

make-up, eyelashes blackened with mascara and lips crimson with lipstick. Normally they were not allowed any make-up. As for Daisy, who was not wearing dark glasses but had her eyelids made up with black crosses like those of a clown, she looked strangely fetching as well, her cheeks rouged and her lips gaudily smeared with red.

After knocking with a broomstick on the wooden floor, Cedric, wearing tails and a top hat, announced, "Ladies and Gentlemen, let me introduce to you the one and only Bottomleigh House Gang in their latest production: Murder of a corpse!"

Then the hilarious romp they had prepared started in earnest. The "young people" performed it with great gusto and had everyone in stitches by the time they ended up in a spectacular pile-up of corpses. The show was enthusiastically applauded.

The next day, when the sun had given ample proof that it was back for the duration, they all convened in front of the garages again and took out the bicycles. And that is when William showed up with his new invention. What he held in his hands were two cigarette cases, of the sort manufactured out of heavy cardboard to look like shiny black leather. But the "devices", of course, were hidden inside.

"I know that Daisy gets very tired from the effort of navigating by ear," William started his explanations. "And the rattling playing card is no good either, as it is noisy and irritating. Then, at the shooting range the other day, I had an idea. We need to produce a distinctive signal at a distance just as with the brass bell..."

The first cigarette case had a push-button mounted on it and contained a miniaturized radio transmitter. "Nothing fancy, just a single frequency oscillator, in order to produce a simple on-off short range signal. It's based on the smallest radio valve in existence, the so-called micro-tube, and of course it's powered by a hearing aid battery."

"Of course!" Daisy said. "You sound very modest about it, but I must say I have never heard of such a tiny radio transmitter before."

The other case had a radio receiver inside, connected to an electric buzzer that one could hear through a cluster of little holes punched into the lid. With a couple of rubber bands for each, William tied the first box to one of the handlebars on Daisy's machine, and the second one to his own bicycle. When Daisy pressed the button on her device, incredibly, it was the other one, on William's bike, that produced a strange beep, like the hoot of an unearthly waterfowl. "Now you get the idea," William said. "I'll make sure I stay in front of you at all times, and you only need to activate the buzzer briefly, and you'll know exactly where I am."

"That sounds great! And how would you call this invention of yours?"

"A Remotely Controlled Signalling Device?"

"That's rather a mouthful, and hard to remember. Why not call it a *remote*, quite simply?"

"My dear Daisy, you may call it as you like. I built it especially for you, and you may have it for keeps."

"Oh, thank you! A *remote* it is, then."

And it worked like a charm. Daisy found it much easier to focus on just one point in front of her to navigate the road, and of course it was very convenient to have that point provide a signal exactly when you needed it. But what's more, she would also receive confirmation of the where-abouts of all the others, because each time she pressed her button, and William's handlebar produced its unearthly hooting sound, the whole gang would burst out in giggles.

And so it had gone on for a couple of weeks in the summer of 1939. In general, the young are not aware of it in the moment itself, but later on, in retrospect, they discover that those summer holidays of years gone by constituted a heart-rending glimpse of a lost paradise that can never be recaptured... Especially in that year, for not long after the end of the holidays, in September, Poland was invaded by the Nazis and the Soviets, both very much in cahoots. And by the time Daisy turned seventeen, the world went to war for the second time in twenty-five years.

III   1943: The funeral

Daisy lived in the dark, though she could have argued that a blind person is never in the dark. But at her flat in Tufnell Park, all the windows were blacked out permanently.

Long before the German bombers had appeared in the skies of London, the population had been told to black out every window of every home at night. The first orders to that effect had been issued at the beginning of September 1939, even before the war was officially declared. Streetlights were switched off or dimmed, shops had to install two curtains at the door, one behind the other, to prevent light from escaping as customers arrived or departed. The blackout soon proved to be one of the most inconvenient measures at the outset of the war, disrupting everyday life for everybody before a single bomb had fallen. Another inconvenience was the requirement to carry a gas mask in a shoulder bag at all times. There was widespread grumbling, but no one dared to question the necessity of these measures.

For Daisy all this had made no difference, or very little. At the time she had just lived on quite happily in the permanent blackout that had been her world ever since she was born. Even when she forgot to take along her gas mask, which happened often, no policeman or air raid warden dared reproach a poor blind girl, and they left her alone. When those first orders were issued, she had been in love and living with her head in the clouds, lost in delightful thoughts. Of course she had still been at home in Barnsbury with her parents at the time, or at school, where the war affected her even less.

Sitting in her darkened living room on the second day after Ralph's death, Daisy sipped her tea and thought back to the time when they had moved in together. Ralph had said, "I've dreamed of this all my life. A simple little flat in London, in an ordinary neighbourhood on the outskirts. To just share a modest home with my lovely wife, away from the social constraints of manor life... You have no idea how endlessly I fantasized about this."

"And did you ever imagine that the girl you would marry would be blind?

"No, of course not. That came as an unexpected bonus..."

"A bonus, really?"

"Yes, and the bonus is, that you opened up a whole new world for me."

"Well, isn't that what a girl is always supposed to do for her lover?"

"Yes, but I'm afraid it rarely happens! Apart from doing just that in bed, obviously..."

Oh, how delightful it had been to move in together! They'd had no other honeymoon than to hole up in their poky little flat and make love as much as they wanted. They had done that with the intensity of despair, because after ten days Ralph had to go away to start his Cadet training.

But it was also very strange to be married, all of a sudden. A few weeks before their wedding, Daisy had confided to Ralph, "One moment you're just a girl, you know: attending a boarding school, doing your A levels. Then you turn eighteen, and a few months later you're supposed to be a married woman, setting up your own household."

"I know," Ralph had replied. "You're much too young to be a bride, and I to be a bridegroom. The only reason I asked you to marry me, is that I want to be allowed to make love with you..."

"Well, and how do you think it feels to receive a proposal from a man who maybe has only a few months to live?"

"Then let's make the best of the little time we have, as the convict said on his way to the gallows."

At that time Ralph had just adored gallows humour. It was at the beginning of 1941, the Battle of Britain had come and gone, and had been on the front pages and on the wireless for months. Everyone was aware of the fact that RAF pilots did not live long. Even going through the pilot training programme was hazardous in the extreme. Then the Blitz had started, and everyone who stayed on in London felt likewise that life could be snuffed out at any moment without any forewarning. Furthermore, when Ralph had started flying his first bombing missions over enemy territory, the feeling of impermanence became even more acute.

"How can you stand it?" Daisy had wondered. "The idea that each mission could be the last!"

"Well, I've volunteered to do this and there is no turning back. And I'm really enjoying every minute of it, one minute at a time. It's like a kind of pact with the Devil: you get to fly the biggest and most advanced aircraft of the age, and in exchange you have to put your own life on the other scale of the balance..."

While Daisy sat reminiscing, there was a knock at the front door of the flat and her mother came in. As always, she was extremely disturbed to find her daughter sitting there in the pitch darkness. "Oh Daisy! Must you really..."

"Mummy, how often do I have to tell you: I'm blind! It

would be a complete waste of time for me to put up and take down those confounded blackout screens every day, so I just leave them up. You may take them down yourself, if that will make you feel better, or else just switch on the lights, please…"

"Darling, I'm so sorry. It just seems so unnatural, that's all. It makes the place so gloomy, so unappealing. All your pretty things, everything so new…"

"My things don't feel neglected at all because of the darkness. I touch them all the time and they feel fully appreciated."

"Well, anyway, how are you doing, my poor sweet darling…"

And at these words Daisy's mother burst out into violent sobs, and her daughter rushed forward to take her in her arms, hugged her and patted her. "There, there, Mummy… I'm all right, really."

Then suddenly Daisy's mother saw her daughter's eyes. "Good grief!" she cried, "that looks awful, darling! Are you having one of those horrible inflammations? Is it because you had to cry? You know that you're not supposed to cry… I mean… better not."

"Well, sometimes one can't help it, can one?"

"I find all of this so awful for you, I can hardly bear it, but you seem to stay so calm…"

"Well, it's not as if it came as a complete surprise, you know. Being married to a bomber pilot right now, you really wait for that knock on the door at any moment. The only thing I would never have expected, though, is that Ralph could become a victim of murder…"

"Murder? Good Lord! My poor Daisy, your grief is leading you astray. It is out of the question, get such a notion out of your head at once!"

"Well, I just received confirmation that Ralph might have died of arsenic poisoning…"

63

"No, no, no! What rubbish, I don't want to hear any more of that! By the way, have you had any news from the Prendergasts?"

"Yes, we talked on the phone this morning. They were just leaving for Essex to go and identify the body. And they are to hire a hearse to bring Ralph's remains back to Bottomleigh, where the funeral will take place. I gave my blessing to all their plans. They will visit later this afternoon on their way back to West Sussex. Maybe we'll go out for dinner together…"

"Well, you could all have dinner at our place, and in the meantime I think you should come home for a while and stay with Daddy and me, until the funeral at least…"

"Mummy, no! We've been through this before, you know very well that I don't want to go home. Or rather: my home is right here. I want to stay where I lived with Ralph. At the moment that is more important to me than anything else."

Right from the start, less than three years previously, the mother had wanted her daughter to go on living with her parents. Daisy was so young. And Ralph was away most of the time. So Mrs Hayes had thought, "Let them use the flat only when the boy comes home on leave; the rest of the time Daisy will only be alone at any rate." But the young war bride had been adamant: she was going to have a new life of her own; her own home; and besides, she was to start her education to become a physical therapist. "That's right, Mummy, a physical therapist… Of course you've never heard of it: it's a very touchy-feely branch of modern medicine. You wouldn't like it one bit. But it's a women's profession, and blind people are welcome…" She had looked forward very much to taking classes of a new kind, together with normal girls of her age.

Just as mother and daughter had reached that point of embarrassing silence when you don't know what to say to each other, the front door opened slowly and an old lady stepped inside. It was Mrs Maurois, the friendly neighbour who lived in the flat across the first floor landing. "Sorry to disturb you, my dear. I heard the terrible news…"

"Mrs Em, *do* come in!"

With a guilty sense of relief, Daisy introduced the two elder ladies to one another. Then without further ado Mrs Maurois stepped forward, folded her young neighbour into her arms and gave her a very French, long, solid embrace. This was unprecedented, but not unwelcome under the circumstances.

"I'm so sorry about Ralph, I loved that boy so dearly!"

"He loved you too, Mrs Em. He liked you very much."

"And how are you coping, my darling girl? If there is anything I can do for you, anything, just say the word…"

"Yes, I will, thank you Mrs Em."

Now the old lady turned to Daisy's mother, her arms wide open. "My dear Mrs Hayes, may I offer my sincere condolences?"

The other woman recoiled in horror. Did this strange creature with her foreign accent presume to touch her? She immediately bid her farewells to her daughter and beat a hasty retreat.

Daisy remained alone with her neighbour, they sat for a while on the living room sofa, holding hands and reminiscing about Ralph. Mrs Maurois also commiserated about Daisy's eye infection; she knew what caused it but had never seen one before. At length, however, Mrs Maurois took her leave, not wanting to impose for too long on her young neighbour.

Beatrice was the next visitor to call on Daisy. The two old friends fell into one another's arms and Beatrice started weeping profusely. Then, after a while, she held her blind friend at arm's length and looked at her eyes. "Oh God, what is wrong with your eyes? Is that ointment or pus?"

"I don't know... probably both."

"Did you go to the doctor with that?"

"No, not yet, but I will..."

Then Daisy's friend took her in her arms again and held her closely. "Oh darling, I'm so sorry..." Beatrice sobbed.

"Hush, I'll be all right. I'll go to the doctor, I promise..."

"No, but I also mean about Ralph... And you're not even allowed to weep!"

"No, but I do weep inside, believe me..."

"And you think he's been murdered?"

"Yes, it looks like it."

"I can hardly believe any of this has actually happened. Ralph is gone!"

"You were in love with him too, once, weren't you?"

"Oh yes, for a great deal longer than you, but only inasmuch as a full cousin is allowed to."

"Oh, Bee, I'm so sorry!"

After a while, when they had both calmed down, Daisy said, "I always had a feeling that you loved me very much, but at the same time there was a bit of tension between us..."

"Well, yes. Do you remember the first time we met? I was moved to tears! I had never seen a blind girl before, and you seemed so *brave*. I just had to kiss you..."

"Oh, I'll never forget that first spontaneous kiss. That made you my favourite out of hand."

"Well, the very next morning I disregarded you altogether and went off with the others. I really thought Ralph would be coming with us, I was hoping to get closer to him now that he had broken up with Cookie. But it didn't work out like that, of course. Then, when we came home at the end of the afternoon, I realised at once that Ralph had fallen in love with you, and I was terribly jealous."

"Sorry for that. You were always the one who was disregarded by all, somehow... Anyway, the reason I called you is also that I need your help. I need a pair of eyes to assist me."

Having said that, Daisy let go of Beatrice, went to the bedroom, and came back with Ralph's little brown suitcase. The two young women settled on the sofa, with the suitcase in between them, and started to examine the contents. "Oh, what lovely pictures of you Ralph had! And one of you two together. And all of them without dark glasses..."

"Exactly. They were made by a professional photographer at a studio around the corner, right here in the neighbourhood... Now, what books did Ralph have with him at the base?"

"*Cold Comfort Farm* by Stella Gibbons, *To the Lighthouse*, Virginia Woolf, *Crome Yellow* by Aldous Huxley, *Brave New World* by same, and *The Story of My Life* by Helen Keller..."

"Ah, yes: Ralph's favourite, that last one..."

"Then there is an *Avro Lancaster Pilot's Technical Handbook*, and these two: *Emil und die Detective*, Erich Kästner, in German, and *Emil and the Detectives*, English translation by May Massee..."

"Yes, Ralph used the original texts of his favourite Kästner books to perfect his German, in case he should need to speak the language if he ever had to bail out over Germany..."

"Good grief, what grim prospects... Well, that's the lot... I suppose he took different books away each time he had been home?"

"Yes, Ralph read a great deal, he found an airman's life rather boring between missions... The funny thing is, he had just read out some favourite chapters from *Crome Yellow* to me not so long ago. He must have wanted to read it again as a reminder of us being together."

"How much he must have loved being with you, darling!"

"Yes... I suppose he did. Now, there is this rough, thickish envelope that seems to contain important papers..."

"Let us see... Wait a minute... Ah yes, you've got that

right, it's a carbon copy of Ralph's will... Drawn up by the family solicitor. You are to inherit all of Ralph's properties..."

"Properties? I had no idea Ralph *had* properties..."

"Well, when he turned twenty-one, not so long ago, he probably came into some inheritances. From old men, vaguely related to the Prendergasts, who died without male heirs. The whole system being based on the idea that women don't count. And then Ralph drew up this will to make sure that his assets, in case he died, wouldn't automatically devolve to some other vague male cousin, but go to *you* instead... At any rate, the listed deeds should represent a tidy little income."

"How clever you are, Bee. I had no idea of all this!"

"No, you wouldn't. *All this* is typical of the world I come from. Be glad you don't know about it... But what this really means, is that Ralph wanted to take good care of you, even after his death."

"Oh yes, how much like him that is. I guess we shall hear more about this after the funeral... But now I would like you to take a look at what seems to be a pocket diary. Are there any appointments in there?"

"Well... yes. Tomorrow and on the same day next week it says EVAC DRILL. And last week and the weeks before... It seems to have been the only recurring appointment."

"Evacuation drill, that's right. Ralph insisted on those. The crew had these extra weekly drills, on top of the compulsory ones."

"You mean like a fire drill?"

"Yes, but in this case they had to drill the evacuation of *D for Daisy*. You see, those seven men are very cramped inside their bomber, there are different escape hatches, and in an emergency they have to get out in a certain order. The skipper is always last to leave, of course. It may also happen that a hatch is jammed and that you need to follow another escape route."

"Wait a minute. Did they actually jump with their parachutes every week?"

"No! No, the plane didn't even leave its dispersal area, but the crew did have to wear their whole outfit, including chutes, and they jumped out onto the ground one after the other. They could do this in fifteen to twenty seconds, even blindfolded."

"Gosh! So, a lot of work for something you'll never need to do if all goes well."

"Oh, but it did save their skins at least once. Their Lanc had been badly damaged by flak, so when they landed, she swerved wildly and keeled over in the middle of the runway, one wingtip ploughing into the grass next to the tarmac. Ralph shouted orders, and the crew rolled out of the hatches like monkeys in a circus act, as Ralph proudly put it to me later, and moments after they had left her, the next landing Lanc crashed on top of *D for Daisy*. That was the end of the first bomber of that name! But anyway. What else do we have?"

"At the end of last week there are some groceries listed. Wine, tea, cream crackers, digestives, relish..."

"Poor Ralph was often feeling peckish, because of the impossible working hours. And he needed a glass of red wine and a little snack just before bed..."

"Did he go out and buy these himself?"

"I don't think so, no. He would hardly have needed a list. Probably the batman did the shopping, and the little list is more of a record to settle the accounts."

"Here it mentions: full tank of petrol..."

"Same story. Ralph and a couple of other commissioned officers shared a car among themselves. They had to keep a record of who had bought petrol when. Especially with the rationing..."

"Now, going back even further, here is something interesting: William's name and address, Bletchley Park,

Buckinghamshire, and Cedric's, some street name in Cairo, Egypt. And Ralph has added: 'send thank-you note'. How extraordinary!"

"That's strange, yes! Not so long ago, we discussed William and Cedric, and Ralph did report that those two were both doing very important, hush-hush work. But he didn't mention that he knew where they were, even though he must have known at that moment that Cedric was actually in Cairo!"

"Well, you know how Ralph was: he would never rat on anyone. 'I'm not at liberty to tell, Sir'. How many times did his father get to hear those words? So he told you the essentials of what he knew, but not the details he was not allowed to disclose..."

"Yes, of course... All right, what else do we have?"

"Essentially more of the same: drills, groceries, petrol. The appointments you would expect for staff meetings and briefings. If you want I can go through the whole diary and read it aloud, with the dates?"

"No, maybe some other time. Now I want you to take a look at the notebooks. Those must contain Ralph's real diaries, in the sense of intimate records, yes?"

"That's right. Pages and pages of handwritten musings, also dated, of course. It will take some time to read all this aloud..."

"That won't be necessary. Ralph used to take the most recent notebook home with him and read his diary to me. The thing is, he hadn't been home for quite some time, and I want to hear the last entries..."

Beatrice found the most recent entries in a notebook that was only partly filled. But to Daisy's great disappointment, she'd already heard those from Ralph himself. "There's nothing new there," she concluded in a trembling voice. "Ralph stopped writing in his diary some time back, probably just after his last visit!"

Then she started sobbing without tears, dry hiccups of despair.

Beatrice cried, "Oh darling, I'm so sorry!"

Daisy had attended a number of funerals since the beginning of the war, starting with that of her dear old Aunt Agatha, an early victim of the Blitz in 1940. For her as a blind person, funerals were extremely uncomfortable and disorienting affairs. You had no idea what was going on, as the whole ceremony revolved around a coffin that everybody could see, but you could not touch. The assembled congregation kept so quiet, that you had no idea how many people were there. You only heard some vague coughing and shuffling of feet around you. Then, after the church service, you all went outside and convened around an open grave, which again you only knew to exist from hearsay. Paying the last respects seemed to involve a lot of restraint and a great deal of distance...

Recently, Daisy had listened with keen interest to a broadcast on the BBC about funerals in southern Europe. She loved this kind of reportage from far-flung places, especially if it included original sound recordings, as had been the case here. It had been clear from the outset that the Portuguese funeral, which had been recorded on a transcription disc by the radio reporter, was a very noisy affair. All the women in attendance wailed loudly and tearfully without pause, and the menfolk muttered continuously in manly tones. They said such things as "Why did you leave us? If only *I* could have gone in your place!" Even the coffin participated in the soundtrack, as the mourners flung themselves at it with abandon, embraced it in their arms and were torn away from it by others, producing a variety of thumping and scraping sounds... No, by comparison, an English funeral was a sedate affair, indeed.

Strangely enough, the village church of Bottomleigh,

now so cold and filled with solemn restraint, was very familiar to Daisy, and associated in her mind with happy memories of that spring morning, only a few years back, when her father had led her to its altar. Ralph had taken her over from him and held her with both arms by his side. This was not what you were supposed to do as long as the vicar hadn't given his say-so, but Ralph didn't care: his bride-to-be was blind, so *there*. The same vicar who now droned on in a monotone, had then been lively and succinct to a fault. What a difference a few years can make!

Of course there were people present today who had not been there on that happy occasion. A few RAF luminaries, and Major Mannings, for instance. And then, at their marriage, a lot of people from the world Ralph came from, the Prendergast relations, the village, had not approved and many had stayed away: a war bride who was not true gentry, much too young, and blind besides! ("Damaged goods...") But fortunately, Ralph's parents had not wavered a single moment in their approval and support of the young couple. They had welcomed Daisy into the family with open arms, and that was the only thing that had mattered...

It had been strange to come back to Bottomleigh House without Ralph. Daisy was given her old room at the top of the first flight of stairs, and her parents the room next to hers. But even though the room was familiar enough, the situation was not. Ralph was dead. A big funeral had to be prepared. Daisy was consulted, diplomatically, and tactfully asked for her opinion and for her approval. And she gave her blessing to everything; of course; how could she do anything else? But at the same time she had the feeling that these numerous preparations went past her altogether; the whole thing was not in the least what she herself wanted; it was as if Ralph's funeral no longer concerned her personally. She would have preferred a very intimate ceremony, a circle around Ralph's coffin, small enough that everyone could have reached out and touched the others…

At least there had been a pleasant reunion with Cookie and Joan, and of course Beatrice was there as well. But on the other hand, who were all these other people staying at Bottomleigh House, whom she'd never met before?

The service proceeded ponderously. After the vicar had finished his eulogy, a number of important men came forward and held long and boring speeches. Daisy's mind drifted off. She decided to think of pleasant memories… The first time Ralph and she had kissed properly, for example. Well, that had been during her very first stay, in the summer of 1939. They had gone to the seashore by bicycle a couple of times, and had bathed in the sea, despite the very difficult, rocky shore. There was a little cove somewhere, where they would go to, with a tiny beach of coarse sand. Daisy could swim quite well, she had learned it at Brighton, and she absolutely loved to go out into the salty waves. Ralph had told her, "You keep smiling and chuckling all the while, Daisy. You really enjoy this, don't you?" Yes. But still, he didn't leave her side for one moment, very anxious and protective. And that she had liked, too. Then on that last occasion, while she waded out of the water, she had stepped on a sea urchin. She cried out in agony. Immediately Ralph was at her side. "Are you all right?" Then, as soon as he understood the situation, he said, "Put your arms around my neck and hold on fast." And he had scooped her out of the water and hauled her across the sand to the rocks. He was a strong boy, but she was not particularly light, so he could only just manage. Then he lowered her carefully, took hold of her foot, and proceeded to pull out the spines. When he had finished, he kept her ankle in his hand, pulled it up, and tenderly deposited a kiss on the arch of her foot where the spines had been. "There, it's over now, you'll be all right." When he let go of her foot, Daisy said "Come here!" She slung her arms around his neck again and kissed him on the mouth. Ralph responded in kind, and after a long while, when they let go of each other, Daisy had sighed, "Oh Ralph! You have no idea how much I like it when you hold me in your arms!" It had been a love declaration of sorts. And it was she who had made it to him, not the other way round...

The speeches had come to an end. The vicar came forward and announced that the coffin would now be carried outside by the appointed pallbearers, and that the congregation was invited to follow them to the churchyard for the interment. There was a lot of shuffling, and they proceeded to leave Bottomleigh Church and headed for the Prendergast family graves. There, Daisy was led to the first row of the crowd, facing an open burial pit that she could not see, but that she knew to be right in front of her. Suddenly she realised that the moment had come: the coffin was to be lowered into the pit. Until now she had undergone the whole funeral passively, as if it hadn't really concerned her, especially as she couldn't weep. But now she felt a kind of panic, a physical, animal feeling that thumped inside her chest. Then she felt a deep anger rising up. She felt she had to *do* something, like one of those southern European widows who throw themselves at the coffin and wail.

Daisy cleared her throat. So far so good: at least it was something. "Excuse me!" she uttered hoarsely. She had been silent for so long, and felt so sad, that her throat had become a bit constricted. She repeated, "Excuse me... I would like to say something." In the meantime her utterances started to cause a stir, people all around her were muttering under their breath, astonished, and some of them apparently rather scandalised. And when Daisy said, "Ladies and Gentlemen, please allow me..." the hubbub around her only intensified. A Portuguese widow would have been quite satisfied. But just when Daisy thought that she was not going to be able to speak because of the agitation around her, Ralph's father spoke up on her behalf, "It's all right, please be quiet. Ladies and Gentlemen, let Daisy speak!" The hubbub petered out immediately, and Daisy began.

"Ladies and Gentlemen, we have just heard many fine words about a young man who was willing to sacrifice his own life, fighting for King and Country. That is all very well. However, there is something important I'd like to say about that."

Daisy's speech had started hesitantly, in a wavering, squeaky voice that she hated. She violently hated this shyness, the girlish insecurity that sometimes overwhelmed her. So she goaded herself on, and as she got into her stride, she managed to speak with more and more self-assurance, almost with authority.

"What I have to tell you is this: even though Ralph was willing to sacrifice his life to fulfil his mission, he did not get the opportunity to do so. He did not die for King and Country. He was not killed by the enemy. He was *murdered* by one of our own..."

Several people started to groan, "Oh no, not that again..." Daisy's own parents, right next to her, were excruciatingly embarrassed, of course, she already knew that. But she had also pleaded with her parents-in-law, and they had reacted exactly like her own mother, repeating almost word for word what she had said: "It is out of the question, get such a notion out of your head at once. We don't want to hear any more of that!" So probably some of these groans came from them... and from Ralph's elder sister, and from other close friends and acquaintances, excluding only Beatrice.

"I'm awfully sorry, but I have to insist. Ralph died of arsenic poisoning. I have a letter right here in my purse, written by a registered pharmacist, who testifies that traces of arsenic are to be found in a Thermos flask that belonged to Ralph. And I myself can testify to the fact that not a single wound could be found on Ralph's body. There is also, to my knowledge, a morgue attendant at Great Dunmow, Essex, who can corroborate that fact. Therefore, I have demanded that an autopsy be performed on my dead husband's body. But I have been denied, not once, but three times. And now I repeat my demand for the last time... There are quite a number of important men standing around this grave here today. Many important men who have the power to do the right thing. It is a power I do not possess, even though I am the widow... So I beg of you, all you important men: grant me this simple wish, for Ralph's sake..."

The speech had come to an end, the plea had been held, followed by a long and uneasy silence around the open grave. And as Daisy started to think that the interment was simply going to proceed without any word of acknowledgement of what she had just said, a solitary voice suddenly broke the silence and rang out. "Oh! this is really too silly..."

Daisy gasped, "Cedric!"

"Let us not be callous, here," the voice continued, with a youthful authority belonging to one who is used to giving orders. "Surely it is not too much to ask that we take a short break, right now? Doctor Westmore? May I suggest that you go and fetch what is required at the village surgery, so that you can take the necessary samples from the body? It only has to be what is needed to determine the presence of arsenic... In the meantime, please, Ladies and Gentlemen, let us all go back to the church and leave the Doctor and the graveyard attendants to perform their task, shall we?"

People started to shuffle. Cedric hectored the crowd, "Yes... That's it... Come on... Let's go!"

Beatrice took Daisy's hand and started to lead her away, Daisy's parents following right behind. Then Daisy felt Cedric's presence at her other side. "Cedric? Is that you, really? I had no idea you were there! No one told me."

"Oh, I have just arrived. I almost couldn't make it on time..."

"And did you come straight here, all the way from Cairo?"

"Good Lord! How do you know about that? It's supposed to be a secret."

"I must say, I'm very impressed, Cedric. You seem to have become quite a leader of men! You even smell different, now: military dry cleaners, the smell of authority! I'm awfully grateful to you for what you just did!"

"Oh, Daisy, think nothing of it! We'll get this sorted out in no time..."

They re-entered the church together with all the other people attending the funeral, but knowing the place quite well, Beatrice and Cedric were able to take Daisy into an outlying corner where they could speak without being overheard.

"How do you know about Cairo?" Cedric repeated. "Did Ralph tell you?"

"No, don't worry, he didn't say a word. But he wrote down your address, and that of William, in his pocket diary. And the other day, Beatrice and I went through that diary, that's how we happen to know..."

"Well, Ralph certainly didn't get those addresses from me, nor from William, I shouldn't think. So please, you two, keep this under your hat, it is highly confidential information."

"But how did you get here, all the way from Cairo? Please tell!"

"Well, as soon as I heard the news, I claimed a seat on the RAF transport that shuttles between Egypt and Britain by way of Malta and Gibraltar."

"Sounds very cloak and dagger! And what about William, couldn't he come away from Bletchley Park?"

"Good God, you know about the Park too, eh? Well, he probably didn't get to hear the news of Ralph's death, you know. At any rate, he's not here today. You see, William is working on a hush-hush project involving thousands upon thousands of radio valves. At Bletchley Park, the best boffins of Britain are building some kind of an electric brain, something they call a *computer*, a device that will execute mathematical calculations thousands and thousands of times faster than any human mind can do it."

"Gosh, I have no idea what that could be like, but for good old William it must be paradise on earth!"

"Exactly. I'm afraid my own job in Egypt is not half as glamorous, even though it is just as important, I can assure you."

"Oh, I can imagine! Just witnessing the way you ordered Doctor Westmore to take those samples from Ralph's body, a moment back: it tells me enough. But now, what happens next? If they find arsenic in Ralph's body, as I expect they will, would you have the authority to demand a coroner's inquest?"

"Well, certainly! That will be the least that they can do! Is there anything else you have in mind?"

"Yes. I would need to get permission to go back to Ralph's RAF station, in order to talk to his crew and his batman..."

"Heavens! That would rather be a tall order! You certainly know what you want, don't you?"

"Of course. We have to get to the bottom of this thing. As I see it, the search now focuses on the person, or persons, who could have put the poison in the flask before Ralph left for his last operation. It has to be someone at the base. And when I hear how you managed to get a seat on a trans-continental transport of the RAF, something tells me that you should also be able to get me access to Ralph's base. No?"

"Well, yes, I might. With a little help from Daddy, per-haps. But there's one thing that would certainly be of some assistance to me in that respect. Could I have the letter from the pharmacist that you mentioned at the grave? It would help tremendously if I could show that to the authorities concerned..."

"Oh, of course, yes. Here it is..."

And as Daisy handed over Mr Dobbs' envelope to Cedric, Doctor Westmore re-entered the church and announced to all those in attendance that the interment could now proceed without further ado. People started shuffling out. When finally all were assembled once more around the open grave, ready to witness the lowering of the coffin, Daisy spoke up again, "Ladies and Gentlemen, as a final tribute to Ralph, I would like to recite a poem he was very fond of. It's the famous *waste-paper basket poem* from *Crome Yellow*, by Aldous Huxley...

"I do not know what I desire
When summer nights are dark and still,
When the wind's many voiced choir
Sleeps among the muffled branches.
I long and know not what I will:
And not a sound of life or laughter staunches
Time's black and silent flow.
I do not know what I desire, I do not know."

IV 1943: Bombing run

Chief Inspector Nigel Cockett saw himself as a happy and cheerful man, mostly. He liked to think that he had every reason to be so. For starters, the Great War had come just too late to maul him the way it had mauled most men of his generation. Born at the start of the century, he had been called up at the age of eighteen, gone through military training, and just when the fourteen weeks of training were done and he was ready to be sent over to be slaughtered in France or in Flanders, the Boche had surrendered with impeccable timing, and the armistice had been signed.

Then, when it had all started again the second time around, he was a policeman. So, luckily, he had been in a "reserved occupation". Very soon the younger colleagues were enlisted in their turn, but he himself had kept just ahead of the age for conscription for senior police officers.

And there you had the third thing the Chief Inspector could gloat over every morning, while he looked at himself in the bathroom mirror and shaved. He had made a stellar career in the police force, not because he was well educated, nor was he especially clever. Nigel Cockett would be the first one to admit with a derogatory chuckle that he was neither.

No, again it had simply been a matter of impeccable timing. Starting on the beat just after the Great War, when police recruits had been scarce and hard to find, then climbing up the ladder steadily and fast, owing mostly to the fact that Great Dunmow, Essex, was the ideal place to achieve this. A small town, few candidates for promotion, but still enough senior posts to be filled. And of course, once the younger colleagues had been called up, this climb up the ladder had led straight to the post of Chief Inspector.

The salary was good; the post came with a car. What more could you ask? Oh yes: and as Chief Inspector, you command authority. Nigel Cockett could afford to be cheeky, stubborn and obnoxious, even towards quite posh people. Him, with his humble origins; nowadays no one dared to tell him off for his total disregard for manners or breeding, that's for sure. Just the other day, there had been this girl, lovely little piece of fluff, though totally blind, banging on with her posh little accent about her dead RAF husband, whining about poor hubby being murdered. What utter rot! He had given her short thrift, that one. He had almost gone too far, he had to admit it. But *she* had slammed the door on him. What a lark!

Then she had sent on a letter, from a London pharmacist no less, claiming that arsenic had been found in the hubby's Thermos. Well-well-well! But still, a Chief Inspector didn't have to act on the whims of a bloody pharmacist... And now, not even a fortnight later, real orders had come down the chain of command to the effect that he, Nigel Cockett, had to pick up the case and get results. It was not only the local coroner's office, it went all the way up to Scotland Yard in bloody London! A post-mortem by one Doctor Westmore had "brought to light" the presence of arsenic in the RAF chappy's corpse. Fancy that! It was one of the few things the Inspector really hated about his otherwise charmed life: you sometimes got orders from above; impossible demands were made by people you could *not* afford to be rude to... "I've never had to solve a murder case in my whole career," the man grumbled, throwing down on his desk the message that had just arrived. "Wouldn't even know where to begin. Not happy at all about this!"

Nigel Cockett sighed deeply, then he took his keys and retrieved his briefcase from under his desk. He put on his coat and hat and went down to the front office. "I'm going for a drive," he told old Constable Kidley. Starting the engine of his police-issue Morris, he mumbled "Let's go down to the RAF station. I'm pretty sure the CO will feel just as miserable to see me, as I will be to see him!"

And indeed, the dead man's Commanding Officer found it "a damn unsettling business." The Chief Inspector did not inspire much sympathy by demanding an office space from the outset, "Otherwise I will have to take people to the police station in town. Your choice, Major..." Reluctantly, the CO took him to a small cubicle that happened to be unoccupied, reflecting that this obnoxious policeman apparently intended to hang around for a while. So, looking sharply at the unkempt civilian who was emptying his briefcase at his new desk, the station commander intoned, "I hope you understand, Chief Inspector, how awkward all this is for me. We have a vital bombing operation against Berlin going on at the moment. It would simply not do to go around the station accusing people of murder..."

"Oh, don't worry, Major. I'm famous for being a real diplomat, if I may say so myself. I just need to talk to the crew that flew with that gentleman on the night he died, and to his batman of course... Maybe a few other people... You know, to get an idea of what exactly happened... But I can assure you that I will go about my inquiries with the utmost tact and discretion..."

"Very well, Chief Inspector, I would be very grateful for that... As for Ralph's crew, as it happens, they are gathered in the officer's mess right now, commissioned and non-commissioned men together. They have a visitor. Let me take you to them at once."

And that is how the inspector came upon a charming, but infuriating, domestic scene, in a quiet and sunlit corner of the station mess. Seven men were sitting in rattan armchairs, chatting agreeably with the blind girl—she immediately recognisable by those horrid dark glasses. Her eyes seemed to be covered with bandages of some sort, but they were well hidden behind the glasses. She was sitting in their midst, with her white cane at her side, holding a tiny model of a bomber between her slender fingers, and the men sitting around her were apparently giving her explanations about it. "There you have them," the CO muttered. "I'll leave you to it..." And he disappeared at once.

"Good God," the inspector thought. "What on earth is *she* doing here? This is really starting to feel like a nightmare!" Then he stepped forward and started hesitantly, "Gentlemen... Madam."

"Chief Inspector!" Daisy cried. "Fancy meeting *you* at the crime scene just a fortnight after the crime was committed!"

The men around her burst out laughing.

"Good Lord!" the inspector sputtered. "How do you know it's me? I hardly said a word!"

"Oh, I'd recognise that voice everywhere: 'This is a case for the Berlin police, har-har-har'."

"Well, I already apologised for that... Anyway, gentlemen... I'm Chief Inspector Nigel Cockett from the Great Dunmow police, and I'm here to investigate the murder of Flying Officer Ralph Prendergast... So let's stop fooling around, this is no laughing matter."

While saying these words the inspector looked down harshly on the group seated around him. He now held the attention of the airmen, who looked up at him earnestly. Only the blind girl kept fidgeting with the model aircraft, apparently engrossed, like a small child at play.

"What is it you have there, Madam?"

"It's a model of a Lancaster that Flight Engineer Derek Wakefield has cut out of balsa wood. Look, Chief Inspector, it has Dinky Toys wheels that can actually turn round... Isn't it the prettiest thing in the world?"

Despite himself, Nigel Cockett did find it rather fascinating indeed. He wondered for a very short moment if he might confiscate this pretty object, but then he thought better of it.

"Harrumph! To order, gentlemen. As I see it, one thing is clear: you were all present at the murder scene. You had opportunity, and, I would say, by definition no alibi..."

"Excuse me, Chief Inspector," Daisy piped up, "but that is rubbish. Ralph was poisoned, so no one on earth has an alibi."

"Did I ask you anything, Madam? At any rate, be that as it may, it doesn't change the fact that you gentlemen are first in line as witnesses... and as suspects. As I see it, who on the crew has motive? The chap who took the victim's place, that's who. The new skipper! The man who got a promotion out of it... So, what I would like to know now, is who of you gentlemen has taken over after the victim's death. Which one of you is it, eh?"

"It's me," said a man sitting in a rattan armchair right next to Daisy. "I understand the logic of your reasoning, but I'm afraid your idea doesn't fly, Chief Inspector. I was not with the others on the night Ralph died. You see, when a skipper is incapacitated or dies, the replacement is always someone from outside the original crew. No one within the crew is qualified to become the new pilot, and I myself could have been posted anywhere else within Bomber Command."

"What's your name, Sir?" the inspector demanded while he took a notebook and a pencil from his breast pocket.

"Flight Sergeant Richard Clayton, Sir"

"Thank you." The inspector scribbled down the name and rank. "And which one of you gentlemen actually took over the controls of the aircraft on that fateful night?"

"I did. Flight Engineer Derek Wakefield. But what has that got to do with anything?"

"That is for me to decide. You are the first one I will ask to make a deposition. Please follow me to my office..."

"Chief Inspector," Daisy interjected, "you do realise that Derek had no need to murder Ralph in order to take over the controls of the aircraft? In fact, he does that all the time. It's normal for the flight engineer to take over from the skipper during a long flight, when the skipper needs to take a rest or go to the 'rest room', for example..."

"Well, Daisy," Derek reflected, "the inspector's reasoning is still valid up to a point, as I am normally not allowed to take off or land the craft. I could still have murdered Ralph, if I absolutely wanted to do a landing on my own at least once in my life..."

"Excuse me!" the inspector shouted. "I'm getting a bit fed up with the meddling and the lack of respect, here. You, Lady, I have a mind to get you expelled from the base. What are you doing here anyway? Trying to solve the case on your own?"

"Not at all, Chief Inspector. I'm only here to have a friendly chat with my late husband's comrades in arms... And another thing: think twice before you lash out at a blind person, and a war widow at that. It might not look so good..."

The inspector sighed deeply. "Mister, er... Wakefield? In my office!"

As soon as the two men had left the mess, the new skipper, Rick, exclaimed, "What a nasty man! My dear Daisy, now I see what you've had to put up with..."

"But tell us honestly, princess," the bomb aimer, Ken, asked. "When you found out about Ralph's death, on that first day, did you really never suspect us?"

"Well, I did consider the possibility, of course... but it's hard to believe that any of you could have done it. I mean to say, *really*... you are the *crew!*"

Ralph had always spoken with a deep sense of awe of the magic of the crew, and Daisy had come to believe in it. It all started with the way a bomber crew was formed.

In a big military organisation like the RAF, you were bound to have a lot of heavy-handed bluster and blundering in the way the hierarchy organised its internal structure and daily functioning. But one unnamed planner within that hierarchy had come up with a brilliant idea, and more remarkably still, he had been allowed to put it into practice. And this stroke of genius, this brilliant idea, concerned the method by which the bomber crews were formed. At the end of the training period, all the specialist trades needed on a bomber were brought together in an Operational Training Unit, an OTU, as a last step before they were sent on to a squadron to fly their first mission. During this period, one day, all the participants in an OTU were assembled in a large hall, the requisite number of each aircrew category being present. But in contrast to the many other briefings and instruction gatherings these men had attended, on this occasion there were no chairs in the room. That was the stroke of genius: people were left to mingle freely, just like at a party or a ball. The officer in charge of the OTU simply instructed the men "to team up". Of course, complete chaos ensued.

"I'll never forget that day, when we crewed up in the 'dance-hall' of our OTU," Sandy Brooks, the navigator, said to Daisy. "That was the very first time I set eyes on Ralph. He looked like Jesus Christ coming straight from the hairdresser's."

"Is that an expression? I've never heard it before."

"No, not an expression. That's how Ralph actually

looked! Seeing him, you just felt that he would know his business, and that he would take good care of you. So I stepped up to him and said: 'Are you looking for a navigator?' And he simply answered: 'Do you know a good bomb-aimer?'"

"Yes, and that's when the two of you came over to me," said Kenneth Rawnsley, the bomb aimer.

"Yes, I knew Ken from the Initial Training Wings, where we had been Air Crew Cadets together, before we were sifted into different trades and went on to our own specialist training."

"And I had Cray in tow" Ken said, "Rear-Gunner Cray Collier, because we're both from Yorkshire..."

"And as the group was forming," Sandy continued, "we were spontaneously joined by Jerry Milton, our wireless operator, and Derek, our flight engineer. The first one from Australia, the other from Canada."

"Then I sneezed spectacularly" Mid-Upper Gunner Timothy Buckley added. "Ralph automatically answered 'Bless you', and I said: 'Do you already have a mid-gunner? 'No', Ralph answered, 'why don't you join us?' And I felt exactly like a fisherman from the Sea of Galilee must have felt on being asked by Christ to join his band of disciples!"

"How well you chaps tell this story," Daisy sighed. "I've heard it before, but you tell it even better than Ralph himself!"

Still, Daisy had come to realize that she could not afford to dismiss the crew as possible suspects out of hand. There were just too few other possibilities; someone at the airbase *must* have poisoned Ralph's coffee on the night he died... She went on fidgeting with Derek's model of the Lancaster because she felt so nervous, and because it allowed her to concentrate on each and every word the crewmembers were saying, without *appearing* to be weighing and analysing their banter for the slightest clue. Daisy sighed discretely and told herself, "I positively *hate* it that *I* should be the one who has to go looking for Ralph's murderer!"

Presently Derek came back from his interview with the inspector. "Good God, what a nasty little man, even though he is tall enough!"

"And who's the next victim that fellow wants to put on the rack?"

"Right now he's talking to the batman. I have the impression that I managed to convince him that my reasons for killing Ralph were rather slim. Now he has put all his hopes on the batman..."

"Of course!" they all sniggered. "It's always the butler that did it!"

"Doesn't that chump realise," the mid gunner reflected, "that in fact the butler *never* did it?"

"What do you say, Daisy?" Ken asked. "Do you suspect Ralph's batman?"

"Well, I just don't know. At least he *is* a key witness. We've already spoken at length, even though he had little time. He's a busy man..."

"But who *do* you suspect? You must have an idea. Do you care to tell us?"

"No one, really. I mean, I have no idea. That's the infuriating thing. *Someone* must have done it. Most probably someone at the base!"

"At any rate," the new skipper grumbled. "We have to put a stop to this inspector's charade. It's almost teatime, and tonight we have an *op* on, for goodness' sake!"

"An op tonight!" Daisy cried. "Are you chaps going to Berlin?"

"Yes, we're not supposed to tell, but yes. We've already had our main briefing, and some of us still have specialist briefings to attend after tea, so I think I'll go and have a word with the CO about this inspector chappy..."

"I wish I could go along with you men," Daisy sighed, and she tenderly stroked the model Lancaster in her hands. "At least we would be able to talk for hours without any interference from that policeman!"

"Are you serious, Daisy?" Rick asked. "Would you be willing to risk your life to come along with us?"

"But of course! Do you think I don't know of the dangers involved? So, what do you say, skipper: may I join you tonight?"

The rest of the crew reacted enthusiastically. "Of course she can!"

"What say you, skipper?"

"It's your call. Let her join us!"

The new skipper had taken Daisy under his wing. At the outset he'd said, "You know, when we fly at night, I believe we're feeling a bit like a blind person, just groping our way through the dark." Daisy was delighted: exactly what Ralph also used to say! She told this new skipper what she'd said to her husband: "The only difference is that we blind people are used to it, and you're not. Being blind is not the same thing as closing your eyes or groping around in pitch darkness."

"I see," Richard Clayton had replied, "but precisely for that reason you could give us night bombers some useful pointers on how to go about this business..."

Now, as Daisy volunteered to join them, and as the crew seemed enthusiastic, he exclaimed, "All right, all right, the majority wins! Good heavens, now I'm starting to understand why *D for Daisy* is such a lucky kite! I guess it would only bring bad luck if we don't take the original Daisy along... I'll go and have a word with the CO."

In the course of the next hours, Daisy's intention to join the planned bombing run to Berlin led to many discussions.

The base Commanding Officer said to D-Daisy's new

skipper, "My dear Flight Sergeant, does the blind girl realise what she's in for?"

"I think so, yes, Major. As I understand it, my predecessor, Pilot Officer Prendergast, had a very open and honest relationship with his wife. He did not believe in sparing the sensitivities of the womenfolk. I heard he was rather candid about the dangers involved in his work..."

"All right. I know for a fact that she is a very spirited girl. What I don't quite understand, however, is why *you* are so keen to take her along, if I may inquire?"

"Well, my concern is for the morale of my crew. They're a rather funny lot: very superstitious about the girl, you understand, what with the bomber named after her and all that... And for them I'm still 'the *new* skipper'... I'm hoping that this little caper will create a better bond between us."

"Very well, I respect that; I will even put it down as a commendable initiative."

"Thank you, Sir."

"But of course you are taking the entire responsibility for all of this..."

"Oh, I certainly am, Major, I certainly am."

Then there was a discussion between Chief Inspector Nigel Cockett and the CO. "I find this highly irregular, Major. What is this girl doing at the base, by the way? Interfering with my investigation? I have the disturbing feeling that she is trying to pull one over on me..."

"Well, Chief Inspector, it's really quite simple. If you want me to put you on that bomber tonight, you only need to say the word... Your request would automatically have precedence over Mrs Prendergast's. I mean to say, a police officer will trump a civilian any time..."

"No, no, don't bother, my dear Major. I think I'll call it a day now. I'll be back tomorrow."

"Hmm, I'm looking forward to that very much, I'm sure, Chief Inspector."

Finally, the crews that were going to fly that night streamed out of their living quarters to be "suited up" at the Parachute Section. The last thing that had been heard from the inspector's investigation, was that the poor batman had been taken into custody. A quartermaster who had his office right next to the Chief Inspector's had heard a loud argument through the thin partition. Allegations and protestations had been flying back and forth.

"You're a bookmaker, you have a criminal record!"

"What has that got to do with anything? I did *not* kill the skipper!"

The humble pen-pusher was delighted to report the end-result of this éclat to D-Daisy's glamorous bomber boys: the batman had been taken away.

All the crews for that night's op were driven out in canvas-topped lorries to the dispersal area, where the bombers were waiting for them, ready for action. The bubbly WAAF driver who "manned" Daisy's shuttle was quite astonished to see another young woman like herself among her passengers. Daisy had removed her glasses, and her eyes were covered with white gauze pads kept in place with sticking-plaster, following her GP's instructions. These big X's pasted over her eyes looked quite dramatic. Now the crewmembers and the other airmen had made a point of not commenting on this, but the WAAF girl spontaneously exclaimed "Ooh, poor thing! That looks awful! And I guess you're tired of living, because of this?"

"No, not at all! What on earth makes you say that?"

"Well, if you're going to get on board of one of those bombers, poor pet, you're in for it!"

"Yes, I know. I'm willing to take the risk, and I intend to enjoy myself. Thank you for your concern..."

"Ooh, no concern at all, darling. You just do as you like, bless you!"

After a short walk they finally reached D-Daisy, parked on her appointed spot on the dispersal area. She loomed large, one of the biggest aircraft of the age, but Daisy could not perceive her size, of course. The men took her over to one of the huge wheels and put her hand on top of the tire to feel its heft. The wheel came almost up to her shoulders. So she could extrapolate the aircraft's size and bulk, somewhat, by thinking back to the Dinky Toys wheels of Derek's wooden model.

The skipper and Derek went on an inspection tour around their machine, going through the check-list they carried with them on a clip-board. In the meantime, the others started hoisting Daisy on board. She was wearing the standard-issue flying suit, electrically heated, with heated boots and gloves, a Mae West life jacket and a parachute. She could hardly move, and giggled nervously as the others literally hoisted her on board, pushing and tugging her along the gangway until they could strap her onto the collapsible seat provided for passengers. Then she was shown how to adopt the "brace position" in case it should be necessary.

"And how will I know that it *is* necessary?" Daisy asked.

"Well, the skipper will be yelling orders like a madman, you can't miss it."

Suddenly an idea struck Daisy: "Say... Tell me... Is it all right that I've never done an evacuation drill... nor jumped with a parachute, for that matter?"

"Don't you worry about that, princess. You're not far from an escape hatch. If we have to bail out, the first crew-member on his way out will unclasp your seat strap, push you forwards, clip your ripcord to a hook and shove you through the hatch. It'll only take a few seconds... After that, all you'll have to do is keep your legs slightly bent for landing..."

"All right... You make it sound so easy!"

"Well, I hope it will never come to that, all the same."

Presently Jerry, the wireless operator, appeared at Daisy's side in order to hook her up to the intercom and oxygen supply. She had to put the bulky leather flight helmet on her head. "In a moment, when we start the engines, this headgear will protect your hearing. The shells over your ears will keep the noise out and allow you to hear what the others are saying. You can even hear us wheezing and gurgling... Then there's the mask that will provide the oxygen you need. The level of oxygen will be raised as we climb to our cruise altitude of 20,000 feet. At that altitude you can't do without, so keep it on at all times. Now, this oxygen mask has a microphone inside, and if you push on the call button, right here, you can speak to the others. But when several people speak at once, it gets to sound like quite an uproar, so that's why you don't speak for too long. Be concise at all times. Give others their turn. It takes some getting used to, but you'll see, we'll be able to chat quite cosily during the flight, just like you wanted..."

"Well, thank you, Jerry. And what if I... erm... need to go to the loo?"

"Oh, ah, yes... First of all you'll have to announce it to the whole company. Then I'll come over, disconnect you, and give you a portable oxygen mask. I'll be sitting right in front of you in my cubicle... And then... Well, maybe now is the best moment to have a little recce on our chemical toilet. Let me unbuckle you... Take my hand and follow me..."

When Rick and Derek finally got on board, they locked the main entry door and had to clamber past Daisy to get to their stations. "Awfully sorry, princess," the engineer muttered.

"That's all right... I'm not really such a princess, you know. I can take the rough with the smooth..."

Then everyone was strapped and ready at their post. The intercom circuits were tested. One by one each crewmember, strapped at his station, reported. At that same moment

Daisy was concentrating fiercely in order to map the whole aircraft in her mind and to pin the voice of each crewmember to the position he occupied. This was a trick she had learned at her school for the blind. "If people at a social gathering are not moving around, you can map their position in the room and pin a voice and a name to each position. That way you'll be better able to follow and participate in the conversations around you." And they had trained to do this.

Richard was the last one to report. "Skipper speaking. All set? Are you all right, Daisy? If you want to get off, this is your last chance..."

"No, I'm staying, really. I'm feeling... so close to Ralph, right now."

Daisy felt a warm glow of gratitude towards the new skipper. What he had just said, that she could still get off, was precisely what she imagined Ralph would have said in the same situation.

"We're delighted to have you with us..."

"Do you often take a passenger along like this?"

"Oh yes. Members of the press, the Medical Officer once, sometimes our faithful CO..."

"Good old Major Mannings!" someone sniggered.

"You see, as base commander, you have to be seen to participate in an operation from time to time. Now, *D for Daisy* has such a solid reputation as a lucky kite that the Major wouldn't dream of taking any other plane... And today we're welcoming the real, the only, the very Daisy who has always brought us so much luck!"

"Hear, hear, skipper!"

"I'll second that!"

"Tonight we'll take you on the journey of a lifetime!"

One by one the engines coughed into life and started humming endlessly. All manner of mutterings went back and forth through the intercom, still concerning the check-list for take-off, but there was also a lot of nervous bantering. Then at last the flag signal was given by a man on the ground outside. Radio traffic was kept to a minimum: you didn't want to give away the game to the enemy. It was now their turn to roll off the dispersal area and take their position in the line of Lancs lumbering to their starting position at the head of the runways. Daisy could feel the wheels wobbling over the grass of the airfield. After taxiing like this for a while they finally reached the tarmac. A tanker lorry was waiting there to top them up with petrol at the last possible moment. And then it was their turn.

The take-off of a fully loaded Lancaster bomber was a terrifying experience. Four Rolls Royce Merlin V-12 super-charger engines, roaring at full throttle for endless minutes, produced an overwhelming din. The four-fold thundering, at very close range, went through the metal innards of the aircraft and right through the bones of each of its occupants. The flight engineer had to kneel down next to the pilot to help manage the throttles as the bomber hurtled along the runway, trying to pick up sufficient speed to get its 26 tons into the air before running out of tarmac. The engines could take such punishment for only five minutes before over-heating and seizing up.

What Daisy couldn't see were the flames coming off the exhausts, eight parallel streams of fire licking over the top of the wings, four to each wing, right next to the more than 2,000 gallons of pure petrol that were stored in the tanks inside those same wings. What Daisy was not aware of, either, were the miles of copper conduits containing highly inflammable hydraulic oil for controls and flaps and gun turrets, altogether 150 gallons of oil. Then there were six tons of lethal high explosive and pyrotechnic stores in the bomb bay, and 14,000 rounds of ammunition in aluminium alloy tracks extending along the fuselage to guide the belted ammunition to the gunner's turrets. There were oxygen ducts, electrical wiring, intercommunication lines and a host of other fittings closely packed together all around you. A highly explosive behemoth hurtling through the night to the end of the tarmac strip...

At the side of the runway that was brightly illuminated by floodlights, visible only to those crewmembers who at that moment could look out of a gun turret, there stood a small group of ground crew and WAAFs who waved farewell to the departing bombers. A little ritual they had in all of Bomber Command. Sometimes even Major Mannings stood there and saluted, but from a departing bomber you could never make out if it was really him.

As she got up to speed, D-Daisy started to shake and rattle like the hapless victim of a spasmodic fit. Finally, after what felt like ages, they were airborne, climbing slowly and circling into their allotted position within the bomber stream. Then they headed out over the North Sea.

"Time to ditch those extra bombs, skipper!"

"Dream on, wireless, dream on..."

"What extra bombs?" Daisy asked into the oxygen mask while briefly pushing her call button.

"Well, for the raids on Berlin, Bomber Harris has ordered us to take on an extra two thousand pounds. Of course that puts rather a strain on a four-hour flight over enemy territory... The rumour goes that some skippers just ditch those two thousand pounds in the drink..."

"Would Ralph ever have done a thing like that?"

"Oh, no! He was a stickler for obeying orders, just like the new skipper here..."

"And is that bad, Tim?"

"No, not bad. Don't take everything we say at face value... But really, if this rumour were true, it would reflect rottenly on those who did it; I wouldn't want to be part of such a crew..."

"Why not?"

"Wrong attitude... very unprofessional. You wouldn't survive for long with such rotten morale."

"So Ralph had the *right* attitude... but he was learning German!"

"Weren't we all?" Derek cried. "I'm still doing my *deutsche Übungen* faithfully! Why would that be wrong?"

"I'm not saying wrong... But Ralph told me you were all dreaming of becoming prisoners of war."

"Yes! *Stalag Luft* prison camps! The only legitimate ticket to survive the blasted war! But that was not at all in a defeatist spirit, you know..."

"Someone tell Daisy about the time Ralph made us dismantle our own aircraft to get us home."

"Ah yes, well. Let me start the story. On that day we were badly smashed by flak: two engines on fire, outer starboard and inner port... Derek activated the automatic extinguishers, but one engine just kept burning."

"Right there we had legitimate reason to bail out, and could have done so without risking our lives."

"But the skipper, Ralph, told us to hold on to our hats and went into a steep dive, to try to blow out the fire in the slipstream..."

"And it worked, too. But by the time he'd pulled up level again, we were flying very close to the ground, on only *two* engines..."

"Again, we would have had every right to bail out!"

"Now we needed to regain some altitude urgently."

"Because we could have been shot down by any angry German with a hunting rifle..."

"So Ralph told us to dismantle and throw overboard as much dead weight as we could."

"We jettisoned the guns, the ammunition, the Elsan toilet and everything else we could unscrew and shove through the hatch..."

"And so we limped back all the way to England."

"No radio to warn them ahead..."

"As we landed, we swerved and keeled over on the runway."

"And that is when we were finally ordered to bail out!"

"We ran off like rabbits into the bushes, moments before the next Lanc crashed on top of us."

"That part I've heard from Ralph," Daisy cried. "Even on that second Lanc no one was hurt in the end, and the next ones coming in had enough time to abort their landing!"

"Exactly! And later that morning we slept in our own beds... But you see, we were never going to relocate to a Stalag on a whim."

"But should it ever become inevitable, we'll be ready, and looking forward to it..."

Presently the skipper announced, "People, in the meantime we've come in range of the enemy. Gunners, all navigating lights are off."

But of course the gunners, always on the look-out, had already noticed that the other Lancs in the bomber stream were no longer visible in the dark. They peered intently into the night sky, searching for the even darker silhouettes of the other bombers, ready to raise the alarm if any of them came too close. In the denser bomber streams of that winter of '43-'44, the crews were very nervous about the possibility of mid-air collisions with friendly aircraft.

"Now, we have some work to do," the skipper said. "Navigator, give us some figures." There followed a lengthy exchange of figures and technical information from the navigator, the flight engineer and the wireless operator. The bomb aimer gave a run-down of the bombing instructions *D for Daisy* had been assigned. Daisy didn't understand a word of all this, but she didn't mind at all. She was reflecting that not so long ago, it would have been Ralph collecting and assimilating all this highly abstract information... She felt certain that he must have been very good at this.

She also mused on the fact that this intercom system was ideally suited for the blind. You just heard the others speaking right inside your head, effortlessly, without having to prick up your ears; and with those muffs on, and the leather helmet around your scalp, you felt protected, comfortable. It was also ideally suited for polite and agreeable conversation, because only one person would speak at a time, and everyone was listened to in equal measure. Meanwhile the engines were droning on and on, in such a monotone that you no longer heard it.

At length, the technical consultation petered out, but then the intercom silence was broken by the bomb aimer. "But please tell us, Daisy, what exactly did Ralph's batman say? You said you'd spoken for a while..."

"Well, yes. The sad truth is, everything he told me incriminates him. And he's very much aware of that. His name is Victor Hadley, by the way... Victor told me that he always prepared Ralph's coffee himself, personally, percolating it directly into a preheated Thermos, and then putting it in the bag Ralph took with him on the plane... He just can't understand how anyone could have put poison in the coffee on that fateful day... He feels terrible about all this, absolutely devastated. And even though I can't afford to exclude him as a suspect, I just had to feel sorry for the man. I told him not to worry, that there must be an explanation; that no one can accuse him, just because he was doing his job the way he should..."

"Hmm, try explaining such subtleties to the likes of Chief Inspector Nigel Cockett..."

"I know, it doesn't bear thinking about, does it? But then, when we were suiting up at the Parachute Section, it suddenly struck me... with all the different crews milling around there, retrieving their gear and putting away personal possessions... the murderer could easily have taken advantage of the confusion to poison the coffee there, at that moment..."

"Good thinking, but still it is hard to believe that anyone of us, I mean from *any* bomber crew, could have done such a thing."

"Agreed. But at any rate, it's good to be able to come along on this flight."

Suddenly the navigator announced that they were flying out of range of the radio beacons back home. He transmitted the coordinates of his last readings. Then there was a brief discussion to determine whether or not they had already passed the Dutch-German border. The skipper concluded, "However it may be, we'll soon be inside the Reich if we're not already there... And I don't mind the chatter with our charming guest, but for God's sake, gunners, keep your eyes peeled, and wireless, keep your ears peeled!"

The crew reacted with derision. "Aye Aye, Sir!"

"We're not stupid, you know..."

"Nor are we suicidal!"

"All right, all right! I'm sorry I mentioned it! I'm just a bit nervous, that's all. We've had an awful lot of luck up to now..."

After that no one dared to speak, and Daisy thought it wiser to wait until someone else said something first. At length it was the skipper himself who broke the silence.

"So, Daisy, we were saying that it's good for you to get an idea of how we fly an op..."

"Yes, I'm trying to imagine exactly how things went on that fateful night, and this is certainly the best way to do it. That's why I'd like to talk about Ralph's last op in particular. For those who were there, you must tell me all you can remember. For starters, was there anything out of the ordinary going on?"

"Well, there was, now that you ask," Derek said. "Ralph should never have been flying on that night..."

"Really! Go on... Why not?"

"He wasn't feeling very well... Upset tummy... You know... aches, feeling a bit sick... Nothing dramatic, but he just wouldn't go to the Medical Officer with it, because he was afraid of being grounded."

"Being grounded for an upset stomach just wasn't Ralph's style," someone commented.

"But in this case I was a bit annoyed, because it meant that I would have to take over the controls a bit more often than I would normally do..."

"Ralph was having to go to the Elsan toilet *a lot*..."

"Wait a minute... Why has no one ever mentioned this before? This is incredibly important!"

"No one has ever asked! Until that inspector turned up this afternoon, the whole thing has never been discussed with us."

"And then what happened?"

"Well, it was all right, although Ralph was very quiet. And apart from the problem our rear-gunner just mentioned..."

"The mood was a bit subdued, but altogether we had a very successful run that night."

"Yes, we dropped our bombs without too much trouble and headed back..."

"But then we hit a flak barrage, just as Ralph was holed up at the back again. *I* had to fly us past it. Normally you have to weave like mad to make it harder for the enemy to hit you..."

"Although you sometimes weave straight into an upcoming shell!"

"Yes, what is called an unlucky weave..."

"At any rate, I'm not proficient at weaving a Lanc through flak, so we had some heavy going while Ralph was away."

"Then we were in quiet waters again, and there was still no sign of Ralph, so I left my wireless cubicle to investigate, and I found the skipper lying on the gangway halfway down, not so far from where you're sitting right now, Daisy..."

"Was he still alive? Was he conscious?"

"Yes, he was at first, but he wasn't making sense. As soon as I'd connected him to the intercom, he said to us 'I'm so sorry, chaps... I don't always know what I want'. Does that make any sense to you, Daisy?"

"Oh yes! I think it's something from a poem... How extraordinary! And then what?"

"He soon lost consciousness, and I carried him over to the rest bed of the first aid station, right behind you, and I connected him to the oxygen and made him as comfortable as I could."

"By that time we were rather in a panic, or at least *I* was, because it looked like I was going to have to land *D for Daisy* by myself at the end of our run, which I'd never done before."

"Well, you did all right, engineer, outstanding job!"

"Hear, hear!"

"You saved the day!"

"Thanks, guys. Well anyway, as soon as we'd landed, Ralph was rushed to the infirmary. We still assumed that he was going to be all right..."

"After debriefing we went to bed, and when we woke up at the end of the afternoon, we were told that Ralph was dead..."

"That is, in a nutshell, what happened that night."

"Thanks, I'm starting to get a clearer picture... But didn't anyone of you find it strange? I mean to say, what had happened was really bizarre, when you stop to think of it."

"With hindsight, yes. But at the time we were assuming that Ralph had been killed by shrapnel from the flak. You know, the kind of tiny unlucky bit that sneakily hits a vital organ..."

"And we were assuming that the medics had sorted things out, determining the cause of death and so on..."

"We were making a lot of assumptions..."

"And of course it's a tribute to you that *you* found out that Ralph was murdered, and that his coffee was poisoned."

"Strange that it had to be a blind person who discovered that..."

The conversation petered out and again the men exchanged some technical communications, while Daisy thought over what had just been said.

After a while Jerry asked, "Do you want some coffee, Daisy?"

"No, thanks. I think I'll avoid drinking until I've eaten my sandwiches. I don't want to have to use the chemical toilet more often than strictly necessary..."

"Wise decision," the rear gunner said. "You do realise that it is just sitting there in the gangway, no closet whatsoever?"

"Yes, Jerry has shown me the set-up before we took off..."

"And still you decided to stick around... That I call steely resolve!"

"But tell me, by the way: is it normal to offer one another a cup of coffee during the flight?"

"No. Each one of us tends to stay at their own post during the whole flight..."

"So normally each one of us sticks to their own Thermoses."

"Especially as you have to keep them closed and anchored at your own station at all times. The skipper may need to weave or dive at any moment, so it wouldn't do to hand over tumblers of coffee among ourselves..."

"But really, Daisy, are you wondering if one of us

handed Ralph a cup of poison? Wittingly or unwittingly?"

"No! Of course not. The arsenic was found in Ralph's own Thermos, so that's completely out of the question... But now that you mention it, I had a strange thought just a while back, and as I want to keep everything above-board, I will tell you what I was thinking. There is only one way that you chaps could have been involved in poisoning Ralph, and that would be if you all had been in it *together*. You know? Like in *Murder on the Orient Express*. A conspiracy!"

"Good God, what a nasty thought!"

"I know, I know..."

"And why would we have done such a thing?"

"Because of your ticket to the *Stalag Luft*, for example. This whole idea crossed my mind when you were telling me about that. What if Ralph stood in the way of your only legitimate ticket to survive the war, and you all decided to do away with him? Not that I really would believe such a theory, but it just crossed my mind..."

"Would I be involved in this conspiracy?" This was the voice of the new skipper.

"Well, not at the beginning, of course. You weren't even there at the time of the murder, but you might be involved now..."

"I see... Yes... It makes perfect sense. And if I'm not involved I might become the next victim!"

"Yes, and it would go on like that until the conspirators found an amenable skipper!"

"You know, Daisy," Jerry now said, "seriously, if I were you, I mean, in your situation, I wouldn't hesitate one moment to mention this possibility to the police."

"Yes, you may be right, except that in this case the police means Chief Inspector Nigel Cockett. I wouldn't want to muddle his mind even more!"

The men chuckled over the intercom. Then Daisy continued, "No, I'll just focus on that Thermos without thinking of the culprit—or culprits—any further. It drives me crazy..."

"It strikes me now," Ken reflected, "that we might be having a little misunderstanding on one particular detail. You seem to assume that Ralph had only one Thermos. But he actually had *two*..."

"We all have two Thermos flasks on a long flight like this."

"When we started flying to Berlin, eight hours or more at a stretch, we doubled our stock of coffee and got to taking along enough sandwiches to last all night..."

"So one flask for the way out and one for the way back."

"Really? And are you sure that Ralph had two flasks of coffee on his last bombing run?"

"Actually, no!" Derek called out. "I seem to remember that he took only one that night, presumably because of the upset stomach."

"All right, but normally he would have had two?"

"Yes, since the start of the long-range ops..."

"Now, the strange thing is, when I came to the base to pick up Ralph's affairs, I was handed only one Thermos flask. So what happened to number two?"

"Is it important?"

"It could be... Actually, it could turn out to be crucial. It may be the piece of the puzzle that was missing until now, but that could lead to the answer!"

"How's that?"

"Well, just think. What if someone stole that Thermos? I mean, the murderer? And he didn't realise that he had to take away *two* flasks, if he wanted to get rid of the evidence?"

"Yes, but if the murderer had put the poison there in the first place, he would have known that there were two flasks..."

"Oh... Yes. That's right... But still, the fact remains that I received only one flask, while Ralph had two of them. And I have to assume that the one I have is the one Ralph took along that night, as it contains traces of arsenic. Then what happened to the other one? Well, I'll have to ask Victor about that. Maybe it will turn out to be another case of a question nobody asked, while the witness knew the answer all along!"

"Yes, it certainly is puzzling, this…"

As everyone thought this over, there was a lull in the conversation. Then for a while only some business-like mutterings fluttered back and forth through the intercom. A coded message came through on the wireless, ordering a small change of course, probably to avoid a strong flak location in front of them. The navigator set to work and transmitted new coordinates to the skipper… And the engines droned on.

Meanwhile, Daisy reflected that her trip on the bomber was already proving to be fruitful. There were now two pieces of the puzzle lying in front of her: two details in the course of events that were highly unusual, irregular, waiting for an explanation. She thought, "I wonder if the Chief Inspector has gotten this far… Maybe we should compare notes after all, when I get back… *If* I get back… On the other hand, I would have to admit that I am trying to solve the case on my own. 'Well, Chief Inspector, I lied to you about that!' No, better not."

Suddenly the excited voice of the wireless operator instantly jolted everybody. "Night fighters! They are probing us with their Lichtenstein radar!"

"Very well." The skipper said. "Prepare for action. Daisy, brace position!"

"All right!" Daisy leaned forward with her elbows on her knees and her head between her arms. She waited. The Lancaster started weaving, tossing her left and right…

Then the rear gunner cried, "I can see one! Fly straight, skipper!"

There was a long burst of loud machine-gun fire.

Then the gunner shouted, "Corkscrew go!"

The skipper shouted, "Corkscrew port go!"

And suddenly Daisy felt as if she was falling, tumbling over into a void. Then it felt like she had crashed to the ground, as in those nightmares where you dream that you're falling. But instead of waking up with a start, she lost consciousness…

The first thing she heard when she came round was "Daisy? Daisy? Can you hear me?"

"Yes, I can hear you," she said. "What was that? What happened? I fainted!"

"Sorry about that," the skipper's calm voice came back, "it's what we call evasive action. It can be brutal."

"It's called a corkscrew" another voice explained. "Diving to port and then climbing to starboard…"

"And this is nothing compared to a good corkscrew *after* we've dropped our bombs!" someone else chimed in. "As we're heavily loaded, the skipper had to go easy…"

"Nice job, skipper, we've lost them."

"For the moment. Stay sharp…"

After a silence, as nothing happened, Daisy asked, "Ralph never told me about such antics. Did he do this kind of thing as well?"

"You bet he did!" the navigator said. "Ralph was the best! He could make a Lanc do things that no one had ever thought possible…"

"That's right, Daisy," Derek added. "Just like you he had incredible sensitive fingertips. But instead of wielding a white cane he was wielding this whole kite with utmost *Fingerspitzengefühl!*"

The skipper said, "We really seem to have lost them… Any readings, wireless?"

"Well, yes. They are still there, they can see us on their screens, but we're not the only prey around, of course…"

"Right. Stay sharp."

Daisy thought it better to keep quiet for the moment. As the corkscrew and her fainting fit had unnerved her a great deal, she made a conscious effort to think of something else than the still imminent danger. She started thinking back to the winter of 1939-40.

She had been in a "serious relationship" with Ralph for several months: nothing unsuitable, adhering faithfully to the rules of propriety. Ralph had stayed with the Hayes family in London a few times, she had been invited to Bottomleigh at Christmas, both families giving them their blessing, with the understanding that they would behave... This didn't mean they did not explore or try to expand the limits of what was allowed. Ralph had taken Daisy to his secret hideout in the basement of his childhood home.

They pretended to go for a walk into the countryside, hand in hand in the bracing winter afternoon, but as soon as they reached the hedge bordering the driveway to the main road they would melt away through an opening that Ralph had known since he was a child. Then they would turn back to the house by secret paths, stealing along the garages and edging close to the side façade of the house, where no one ever came. There they made use of a basement window— the forth from the corner—with a doctored latch that allowed them to open it from the outside and get in unnoticed. Right next to the boiler room there was a cosy, unused little cubicle, with an old mattress and some blankets on the cement floor. They would spend a few hours lying there in one another's arms, petting and kissing, but making sure not to overstep the *letter* of the law that had been laid down by their parents... Then, when they were more or less satiated, they would steal back to the driveway by the same path they had followed on the way in, and pretend to be coming back from a long bracing walk through the winter countryside, their flushed faces due to the cold. Even the old gang, the cousins, had been none the wiser as to where they had been and what they had been up to. And thus they had been quite happy.

Then, during the summer of 1940, Daisy was invited to Bottomleigh House for her second summer holiday. And suddenly the Battle of Britain had started right above their heads, there, in the West Sussex skies. They had heard the Spitfires and Messerschmitt dog-fighting. The gang had enthusiastically described what they could see; on some days the fight had apparently left a spectacular tangle of white contrails in the blue summer sky. And suddenly Ralph's loyalties had become divided. When a battle was going on above them, he would almost forget her presence, Daisy recalled. In the evenings they listened to the reports on the wireless. Churchill, had already styled the events of the summer as the *Battle of Britain* ("The battle of Britain is about to begin") and the broadcasts were accordingly compelling. As a consequence, every lad in the country suddenly dreamed of becoming an RAF pilot, including Ralph, Cedric and William. They all sighed, "Oh! I can't wait to join in…"

Daisy had been appalled. In their secret hideout in the basement, she had asked, "What about *me*? Don't you even want to know what *I* have to say about this?"

"Actually, no, darling. I already know what you think of it. But you *must* understand: we're all going to be called up anyway, so I might as well volunteer for something I *really* want to do."

"Whatever happened to 'I do not know what I desire'?"

"Alas! What indeed?"

Then one day a fighter plane had crashed right outside the village of Bottomleigh, next to the road in front of the King's Arms. When they had heard the news that afternoon, they had taken their bicycles and gone down to the village at breakneck speed. And indeed, the burned-out remains of an aircraft were lying there, even though one could hardly see anything—the others had told Daisy—because of all the onlookers. Besides, the people were being kept at a distance by a policeman. Then they heard that there were some RAF officers having a beer in the pub, so they all went inside. And indeed, a little group of them were gathered at the bar, perched on stools, discussing the crash quietly among themselves. They, the gang from Bottomleigh house, had taken a table as close as possible, but without wanting to appear to be eavesdropping. Then suddenly a tweed-clad local farmer had made his entrance, visibly excited, and he had loudly addressed the officers. "I saw everything this morning! I was literally in the front row for the show!"

Obviously none of the RAF men present felt like talking to this intrusive bore, but one of them was simply too polite to ignore him altogether. "I hope you liked it..."

"Oh! yes. What a terrific fight! Exactly as they say in the papers: our pilots are the best! The Hun didn't stand a chance! What a massacre!"

"Hm," the polite officer mumbled. "I would hate the idea that anyone was massacred..."

"But I'm telling you, I was there, I saw everything!"

"Really? But didn't it escape your notice that the pilot bailed out and made use of his parachute?"

"What are you talking about? The Hun was massacred! He didn't stand a chance!"

"Well, if you'll allow me, I do not share your point of view... The Hun, as you call him, stood every chance, and better still, he was very good. Actually, it was *he* who won the fight, and the other chap who was shot down. Right now, the 'bandit' must be enjoying a nice glass of French wine at a café somewhere in the Pas-de-Calais..."

The local farmer was scandalised by this and stretched his arm towards the open door of the public house, "But what about the wreck, right there, on the other side of the road?"

"Hmm... one of ours, I'm afraid. A Hurricane, you

know..."

"No, no, no! How can you say such a thing! And what do you know about it anyway? I saw everything with my own eyes; I was there, I tell you!"

The RAF chap seemed slightly put off by this. "Now look here, my man: I happen to be the pilot who was involved this morning, yes? I was shot down, and I consider myself very fortunate indeed, as I was able to bail out in one piece!"

Then he chuckled softly, and added, "But of course I could be wrong..."

Ralph was so impressed by this laid-back sense of irony, that he stood up at once, stepped over to the pilot and introduced himself. The man was perhaps so relieved to be rid of the intrusive old bore, that he gladly let himself be drawn into a conversation with the star-struck young admirer! Ralph asked him at once what the secret of a good bailout was.

"I'm not supposed to discuss these matters, you know, but if you're a German spy, your cover is so clever that you deserve to know all you want... It's quite simple, really, at least in theory: open canopy, unstrap self, turn aircraft upside down and drop away... Of course the canopy might jam, and you might get badly burned if the engine in front of you is ablaze, but this morning I was lucky. Everything went by the book."

"And do you rehearse this procedure a great deal?"

"Of course! Every good pilot does. But never in combination, obviously. You train the unstrapping without opening the canopy; the opening of the canopy without unstrapping; and turning over the aircraft without executing the two other moves..."

"And by training all that regularly, you put all the chances you can on your side..."

"Precisely! You've got that in one."

Thinking back on this episode Daisy still marvelled at

the fact that people with eyesight could be so full of themselves like that Bottomleigh farmer, so proud of their powers of observation, and still be utterly misled by their own eyes! At any rate, after this friendly conversation with the downed fighter pilot, Ralph's fate had been sealed. Not only was he going to volunteer as soon as possible, but he would be a pilot, and a good one at that. Only, it turned out that by the time he became a Flight Cadet, fighter pilots were no longer needed, only new skippers for the bomber crews.

Finally they reached Berlin. The area was a cauldron of activity: searchlights sweeping the skies everywhere, flak barrages so dense and extensive that there was no way of evading or bypassing them. And of course, right behind the flak the place was swarming with German fighters having a field night. The intercom came alive with exclamations from the crewmembers who had a good view ahead: the skipper, bomb aimer and mid gunner.

"Good God, there's a party going on!"

"Hold on to your hats, we're joining the scrum!"

"Flak ahead! Flak ahead! There's no avoiding it!"

The sound of shell explosions outside the aircraft became louder and louder; the bomber started to shake; shrapnel hit the fuselage like pebbles thrown violently against a windowpane. Daisy froze in her seat, mentally bracing herself: this was the deadly lottery Ralph had often mentioned, where chance alone determined how much damage an aircraft and its crew would sustain. On the other hand, Ralph had also explained, you had to trust the laws of physics, the inverse-square law: the intensity of a burst of shrapnel should be inversely proportional to the square of the distance from its source—the exploding shell. Only very close strikes were really dangerous. But still, some bombers were unlucky and took a full hit.

At some distance from them, another Lanc suddenly

exploded, all of its bomb load and what was left of its fuel igniting at once. They heard a tremendous boom. The sky around them was briefly illuminated by a burst of erupting flame spreading forth at 180 knots, the flight speed of the bomber. "Good Lord! Those poor chaps certainly went off with a bang!" the skipper cried. "There's no way anyone could have survived that!"

A tense voice commented, "You know, Daisy, right now you're lucky to be blind. There are some things you'd just rather not see..."

"I know, Tim, this is certainly one of them..."

Then several of their machine guns started firing at once, and as soon as they stopped shooting *D for Daisy* lurched violently in another attempt at evasive action. "Careful skipper, bombers and fighters all over the place!"

"We'll just have to take our chances!"

"Welcome to the scrum!"

Again, the inverse-square law... hopefully.

Until then the bomb aimer had been seated at the machine-guns in the nose turret. Now he had to lie down on his belly, with his head inside the large transparent Perspex nose cupola, the bomb-sight *computor* on his left, the sighting head in front of him and the release selectors on the right.

D-Daisy was flying at the front of the bomber stream that night: a doubtful honour bestowed on the most experienced crews. This meant that they had to wait for the *pathfinders* to drop their flares; the pathfinders being mostly nimble twin-engine Mosquitoes that reached the target area in advance of the heavy bombers and marked it with a grid of brightly coloured flares. The bombers coming in later only needed to drop their loads on an appointed location within the grid, but the early ones had to wait for a while and circle in the dangerous skies above Berlin...

"Target indicators going down!" the bomb aimer exclaimed. "Can you see them, skipper?"

"Yes! Shall we head there now?"

"Certainly! Let's get on with it... Our target is somewhere between the green and the red markers. Let's have a look."

Ken started to give indications to the pilot, "One point five to port... straight ahead... half a degree starboard... half a degree back to port... beautiful."

This was the most dangerous part of the whole operation: as you neared the target your course became quite predictable for the enemy flak gunners and the fighter pilots. Before actually dropping the bombs you needed at least ten seconds of straight flight to allow the aimer to pinpoint the target in the sight optics. Ken announced, "Bomb doors open!" and after the skipper had opened the bomb bay, a blast of freezing air filled the inside of the plane. "Now keep her straight, skipper, I'll do the sighting..."

After a few seconds Ken exclaimed, "It's no good, skipper, we're too far off target, we have to do a new approach!"

Everybody started groaning, "Oh! No..."

"Ken, please!"

"Just get on with it!"

"Sorry, chaps, we have more wind shear than I could make out beforehand. I'll add a few notches of drift on the computor, and we should be able to do beautifully the next time..."

As they were veering away to turn around, Daisy asked, "Tell, me Ken: is it important to be so precise, knowing that we're just carpeting the whole place with bombs?"

"Important? Only for Ken!" someone laughed.

"Thanks rear-gunner! Are you still having fun back there? But to answer your question, princess: you need to carpet *equally*. If we drop our bombs off target, the next chaps may drop theirs on the exact same spot, which would be a bit useless. And don't forget that we're going to take a photograph... Our harshest critics are those office workers who analyse our photos. Now, skipper, let's start again, two degrees to port..."

At last Ken was able to release the bombs. That is, the release selectors programmed by him beforehand set in motion a stream of high explosives and incendiaries to fall from the bomb bay in the required order. As soon as she was freed of her load, the lightened aircraft leapt upwards and forwards, causing some stomach churning in her occupants. And now they had to wait for the camera flash. After releasing their bombs, they were required to fly straight and level for another number of nerve-racking seconds, in order to take pictures of the bombs striking the ground. With the bomb-load a photo-flash flare had been released, and a timer had been started, which would activate the camera's shutter while the bombs exploded. Then, as soon as the flash had glared below them, the skipper started veering and weaving, trying to extricate them from the boiling cauldron above Berlin. They still had to cross the flak barrages, confront the night fighters waiting for them on the other side, but then, several blasts of machine gun fire and corkscrew dives later, Rick finally was able to announce that they were on their way home.

After about an hour, when things had calmed down, the first one who broke the silence—or rather the monotonous drone of the engines—was Derek, the engineer. "Tell me something, princess: do you know the story of how our Lanc became 'D for Daisy'?"

"Yes! Ralph told me about that first briefing for skippers at the base, after you all had arrived fresh from your Operational Training Unit..."

"It was one of the better ideas of our beloved CO, Major Mannings: to let the pilots themselves choose a name for their brand-new Lancs."

"Only, he simply assigned letters of the alphabet to the men in their seating order, and Ralph was assigned the letter F!"

"He was not happy!"

"So he asked the pilot sitting two chairs ahead of him if he wanted to swap with him: an F in exchange for a D..."

"How could the other guy refuse, when it was asked so nicely?"

"And then," Daisy cried, "you know what happened when he gave the name to the officer who was writing them down?"

"Yes! The chap told him you're not allowed to name your aircraft after your girlfriend... And you tell us, princess, what Ralph answered to that!"

"He put on a straight face and said: 'I don't *have* a girlfriend, Sir, I just want my plane to be named after my favourite flower'... And you know what? Ralph wasn't even lying: we were already married at the time!"

At that they all chuckled fondly. Sandy the navigator remarked, "In a situation like that, Ralph knew how to mix defiance and self-effacement so that the officer just had to let him get away with it..."

"Yes," they concurred, "he was a real diplomat!"

Then Derek said, "I hope you don't mind my asking, Daisy, but was Ralph very posh?"

"Well, actually yes. Eldest son of a squire, to the manor born and all that... After his father's death he would have become the Earl of Haverford, and master of Bottomleigh House..."

"Bottomleigh House?" the rear gunner chimed in. "Me-thinks I'm *sitting* on my Bottomleigh!"

And while he started cackling with laughter at his own joke, the skipper's quiet voice cut him off. "Not funny, Cray!"

"Sorry! Blame the nerves!"

"But anyway," Derek continued, "You'd never have

guessed about Ralph. Even though he did have a posh accent, he was always such a regular guy…"

"That's right. His parents raised him that way. From early childhood on he was taught to respect his nanny, the cook, the gardeners and even the charwomen… Actually, the servants at Bottomleigh House are always called 'the staff', and Ralph's father, who was a Labour MP at one time, insists on being called 'Mr Prendergast'. They're the nicest people I've ever met, Ralph's parents…"

"We all miss Ralph very much," Derek said quietly.

"If only we could find the bastard who killed him!" Sandy exclaimed.

"Yes, I've been thinking," Ken said, "about what we discussed earlier. Not only did Ralph have two Thermoses instead of one, as you were assuming, Daisy, but he also could have been poisoned over a longer period, not just on the day he died… I'm not an expert on arsenic, but I seem to remember something I heard on the wireless about Napoleon. Some experts believe the exiled emperor was poisoned on Saint Helena; that he could have been given small doses of arsenic, which accumulated in his body over time and killed him by delayed action…"

"I also heard that story on the Beeb," Cray said, "only, I can't remember if it was the butler who did it, or the British government…"

"Very funny, again, rear-gunner!" someone protested, but they chuckled all the same.

"No, but seriously," Ken insisted. "This could be significant."

"You're absolutely right," Daisy said. "When Derek told us that Ralph was feeling very sick on the day he died, I started to think along the same lines immediately. And I'll tell you why: Ralph kept a diary, that he read to me when he was home on leave. But when his things were given to me after his death, I found out that he hadn't written anything after his last visit several weeks before... Now this is very strange: he was always writing these messages to me in his diary, telling me how much he missed me, and all of a sudden he stopped doing it..."

They were all silent for a while, then the mid-upper gunner said, "So you're telling us that he must have felt sick for several weeks..."

"Yes. He must have felt awful—and probably quite depressed—to stop writing to me like that!"

"Maybe you're right. It's even quite probable. But Ralph didn't let on, we never knew..."

"If only he had gone to see a doctor!" Daisy cried. "A competent doctor could have diagnosed arsenic poisoning and saved his life!"

"Yes, but there's the rub," Tim remarked. "Apart from the fact that our base MO is probably not experienced enough to diagnose arsenic poisoning, there was no way Ralph could have gone and seen him with complaints such as stomach ache, diarrhoea and vomiting... And you know why, don't you?"

"Yes, I can see where you're going..."

"They're the symptoms of fear."

"Good God!" the others cried. "Medically unfit on nervous grounds!"

"Forfeiting the confidence of his Commanding Officer!"

"LMF! Lack of moral fibre!"

"He could lose his flying badge!"

"The ultimate humiliation!"

Daisy concluded with a trembling voice, "How lonely Ralph must have felt during those last weeks..."

After a long silence it was Rick, the new skipper, who finally asked, "Now what does this tell us about the murderer, Daisy? Do you suppose it is useful information, this?"

"Well, yes. This is actually essential, together with the fact that someone must have stolen one of Ralph's Thermoses without knowing that he was using two of them... I mean, this narrows the thing down quite a bit, doesn't it? And it shows that none of you, nor Victor, the batman, could be the culprit. The murderer was in a position to feed Ralph small doses of arsenic for several weeks, but he was not familiar enough with the circumstances to know about the Thermoses. There's a big contradiction there, wouldn't you say? But if you solve that riddle, you'll know who killed Ralph."

Landing a bomber after an operation like this was not an easy task. The sky around the base was very crowded and you had to wait your turn for a landing order from the control tower, flying circuits while your last drops of fuel were being used up. The aircraft could be badly damaged by flak shrapnel and bullets, and it was not always easy to assess the damage. The ailerons, flaps and rudder could be full of holes.

On the way in, Derek had been peering intently at all the gauges and needles on the control panels, and above the North Sea the skipper asked him for a report. "Flight Engineer, how does it look? Give us the good news first."

"Well, the good news is that all the hydraulic circuits are sound, oil pressure normal; air pressure of tires normal; we should be able to extend the landing gear and land on our wheels..."

"Any bad news?"

"Of course! The usual: we're running low on petrol. I've pumped over all I can into one tank, but I can practically hear those last drops gurgling into the carburettors... If they make us wait too long, we'll have to bail out and chuck the kite!"

"Yes, well. We'll see about that when we get there..."

Finally it was their turn to follow the glide path, slowly yawing and wobbling as they decreased their speed. They felt the rough but exhilarating bump of the bomber touching down and heard the sweet screech of the huge tires on the tarmac. Then, as soon as they had taxied off the runway, the engines were cut back to idling, and for the first time in more than eight hours they no longer heard the steady din of the four engines through their headgear. The light of dawn was just becoming visible for those who could see.

"We've made it, boys!" the skipper said.

"How did you like the trip, Daisy?" someone asked.

"I loved it, thank you, Cray. It was very kind of you all to take me along."

As they walked over to the waiting shuttle, Richard took Daisy's hand and said, "I like the look of that bomber suit on you. It really flatters your figure."

Daisy giggled. "I find that hard to believe, skipper, but how should *I* know? I'm blind!"

"Blind maybe, but not helpless. I admire your courage, Daisy. And you're not unseeing either; I wish you all the best in solving the riddle that you managed to uncover tonight..."

"Thanks."

Daisy, who was almost as tall as the pilot, leaned over and said softly into his ear, "You know, Richard, I'm not entirely easy in my mind about the crew. What do you think: could they be holding something back?"

"Oh no, they're all right, really. But they're a strange bunch... strange sense of humour; gallows humour. I'm not always easy in my mind about them myself."

V   1944: A sinking feeling

The man thought, "Oh Lord, I'm really getting hot round the collar, even though I'm not wearing one!"

He was laying on his back, bare chested, on a padded massage table, and a physical therapist, a woman of course, was energetically kneading the left part of his chest and his shoulder. And the wonderful thing was that her ample but firm bosom was shaking with the effort just one foot from his face. Of course she was wearing a stiff white overcoat, but still...

The man, middle aged, bald pate, his body going to fat, suffered from a persistent electric tingling in his left elbow. So his GP had sent him over to this "physical therapist". Little had he known that this meant a *masseuse*: wonderful! And it had turned out that she was rather shapely and very attractive: even better! And then she happened to be blind; she was wearing a pair of dark, round glasses, and judging by the way she kept her head stiff, slightly turned away from the work at hand, she really had to be totally blind.

This in itself was rather off-putting, of course, but on the other hand, you could stare at the movements of her chest as much as you wanted, and she didn't notice a thing: as blind as a bat!

The man stared and stared. If you looked beyond the girl's dark glasses and the stiff neck, she was actually a quite luscious blonde creature. Even the frown on her haughty brow was attractive in a way. "I know you're hard to get, lady, but I'm ogling you all the same!" It was rather exciting.

The man started fantasising. "Once again I am Caius Lucullus, the Roman patrician, and I have ordered my prettiest slave to come to me and give me a massage... Of course I would have ordered her to take off her clothes, or better still, she would be wearing a very skimpy tunic... And I would put my left hand on her beautiful behind and fondle her buttocks to my heart's content..."

The man gulped. "Oh Lord, I'm getting a hard-on something terrible! It's a good thing that this sexy little number has no way of knowing what on earth is going on..." He sighed deeply. "God, now I really need to touch myself; if I don't give myself some relief, I'm going to burst! Shall I dare to do it? She can't see me anyway..." And just when he slowly, stealthily raised his right hand from the padded table and tried to grope his crotch, the blind girl's hand shot forward and she forestalled his movement. She pushed back his wrist. Then she lifted up the man's trouser front with her left hand, slipped her right hand inside his pants and firmly gripped his erect member in the vice of her powerful masseuse's fingers.

"Are you enjoying yourself, mister?"

"Ouch! Ouch! Stop it, Miss... How on earth could you tell, Miss?"

"It is Mrs Prendergast to you. And if you really want to know: I can read your thoughts... But apart from that: you've been panting like a randy dog from the moment I started my treatment."

"Good Lord, I had no idea! I'm terribly sorry!"

"Well, apology accepted. But keep your dirty mind in check from now on, yes?"

When Daisy got off for lunch, that day, she was feeling very tired and rather depressed. How could the others keep this up full time? She was glad to be working only two and a half days a week. And even that was a challenge. She went out into Hyde Park, not far from where she worked. The early-spring sun was shining, only noticeable to her as a slight and agreeable glow on her skin. She crossed Bayswater Road with a little help from a friendly old lady, then navigated by memory to a favourite bench near the Serpentine, where she wanted to eat her sandwiches.

Hyde Park had become a difficult terrain, with trenches, air raid shelters and anti-aircraft guns. Apparently there were a lot of barrage balloons floating above it, but of course she had no idea how they looked. Someone had told her that they looked like huge sausages... Well, she'd had enough of big sausages for the day.

She found her bench and sitting down she took her sandwiches out of her handbag. She started to munch, and reflected. The incident with the 'pervert' this morning had been a bad turn. She should never have reacted so aggressively. That had been very unprofessional. On the other hand, with this particular man the problem had been solved in one of two ways: either he would never come back, or from now on he would be the perfect gentleman. But it wouldn't do to fly off the handle like that with every indecent patient; she would have to devise a better conduct, a mode of coexistence with such characters. Her favourite teacher at the clinical courses had told the students that they should keep up some small talk, just like hairdressers and beauticians would do. "Talk about the weather, ask the male patients what they do for a living, ask the female patients about their children; things like that..." In the case of the male patients, the idea was that if you kept up the small talk, they would be distracted from any funny ideas. And if they tried to flirt, you could tick them off… verbally. But today, Daisy had to admit, she herself had been too distracted, too preoccupied by other things to function properly. She would have to find a gentler way of dealing with perverts.

"Either that, or I'll just have to strangle all my male patients," Daisy mumbled to herself.

Daisy felt depressed, even while thinking back to her training, recalling the teachers who had made it possible for her to learn this profession, the fellow students who had been sympathetic and supportive. The three girls who had helped her revise for her exams, and all those others. It had not been easy. Before her professional training she had been used to a school where everyone was blind like her. But now she had finally achieved her goal. And for what? Fat, middle-aged men lusting after her? You strive and you struggle, and then, when you reach your goal at last, the long awaited rewards turn to dust between your fingers… It just gave you that sinking feeling.

The same applied to her quest to find Ralph's murderer. After a heady breakthrough at first, her investigation had come to nothing. That was what was preoccupying her; she was thinking about it all the time.

When D-Daisy had landed at Great Dunmow airbase, she had been very eager to talk to Victor, of course. But the batman had spent the night in custody at the police station in town, and he was not back yet. It appeared that he would not be released on that day. Daisy had been very tired after a long and stressful night, and it was clear that she would have to leave the base and find a room at a hotel or at an inn to get some sleep. But before she left, Major Mannings managed to get hold of her and told her politely but firmly that she was not to come back to the base. "I would say that you have had ample opportunity to talk to Ralph's crew during your little excursion to Berlin, Mrs Prendergast. And now the investigation is in the able hands of Chief Inspector Cockett, while I and all the men here have a bombing campaign to run... Do I make myself clear?"

"Of course, Major. But surely you'll allow me to say goodbye to the skipper and the crew as soon as they have finished their debriefing?"

She had only just managed to speak to the men before they themselves went to bed, and through them she had gotten hold of a telephone number that would enable her to get in touch with Victor when he came back to the station. Then she had been evicted.

A few days later, back in London, she had finally managed to speak to Ralph's batman on the phone.

"Victor!" she cried, "How are you? Did you manage to escape the inspector's clutches?"

"Daisy... Yes. I'm fine, thank you. Glad to hear your voice. I need to get back my sanity. Maybe talking to you will help..."

"Of course! Tell me what happened."

"Well, it was quite horrible. The inspector was obviously certain that I am the murderer. He kept reproaching me my background, he kept trying to break me down. He shouted at me, he said that it was useless to deny the facts, that he had more than enough evidence to get me hanged... He told me it would be better for my own sake to confess straight away."

"Oh, poor thing! I hope you remembered what I told you: that no one has the right to accuse you just because you were doing your job..."

"Oh yes, I thought of you a lot. And I came to the conclusion that you are absolutely right. The fool doesn't seem to grasp one small detail: that as long as *I* know I didn't do anything wrong, I have no reason whatsoever to believe a single word of what he says about this so-called evidence... I mean, knowing as I do that I *didn't* do it?"

"Yes, yes, you're absolutely right there, Victor, your logic is impeccable! And so the man didn't ask any *real* questions? He didn't even discuss your testimony?"

"No, nothing of the sort! It was very frustrating..."

And at about that point in their conversation they had been cut off. As part of the wartime rationing, private phone calls were limited to three minutes. Then the switchboard operator would mutter "your time us up," if she said anything at all, and she would abruptly end your conversation. "Drat!" Daisy exclaimed, and prepared to go out. She had to find a public phone booth if she wanted to continue her conversation with Victor. With all the damage from the blitz it was not easy to find a phone in a place like Tufnell Park, and if you were blind it was even worse, but after asking a few passers-by, someone at last was able to lead her to a booth that worked and that was available.

As soon as she got hold of Ralph's batman again, she started explaining as succinctly as possible the conundrum of the missing Thermos flask. "So tell me Victor, Ralph *did* use two flasks, didn't he?"

"Yes, but not on the day he died, that's right."

"So which one did you give to me?"

"The one he'd left behind, definitely. I took it from the cupboard where I had stowed it away the day before..."

"And what happened to the other one?"

"It was brought to me with Ralph's things that came back from the bomber and from the morgue. I put those things on his bed, including the Thermos. I didn't even rinse that one. But by the time you arrived to pick up Ralph's possessions, the Thermos was gone. Then I remembered the other one in the galley cupboard, and I put that one on the bed for you..."

"Any idea what could have happened to the first Thermos?"

"Well, there's a lot of pilfering going on, you know. I

remember thinking that the culprit was probably not aware of having pinched a dead man's flask. That is: this would evidently bring you such bad luck, that nobody who was aware of it would even have contemplated the act…"

"But you don't know who could have done it?"

"No, I've thought about it a lot, but it remains a complete mystery to me."

And then they were cut off again. "Damn, damn, damn!" Daisy cried in frustration. At least this time the conversation had been more or less rounded off, she reflected, there was not much more to discuss, but the outcome was very disappointing. Now Daisy had to find her way back home, which was not so easy, as on the way out she had been briskly guided to a phone booth she was not familiar with. She had to ask for directions several times before she got back on familiar terrain. And when she finally arrived at her place and unlocked her front door, she heard her own phone ringing. She was just in time to pick it up. It was Victor, who at once started talking as fast as possible.

"Daisy! I'm calling from the mess kitchen phone… Listen: something just occurred to me. Do you remember how I told you that Ralph's quarters had to be vacated immediately to make room for another officer? Well, I was saying that because on the very same morning an RAF officer I had never seen before had made a brief appearance to take a look at Ralph's place. He really gave me the impression that he might soon become my new boss. But the funny thing is: he never came back; I never saw him again!"

"Victor! That *is* important information! That man could have been there to retrieve the incriminating Thermos: he could be Ralph's killer. Can you describe him?"

"Yes, yes. Tall and thin with fair hair. In fact, the hair so fair that it looks almost white. And pale grey eyes, exceptionally pale eyes, almost colourless… but good-looking all the same."

"So you would easily recognise him if you met him again?"

"Oh, yes! I would recognise him anywhere, in a crowd of thousands, even. I'm good at remembering a face, and this one was particularly memorable..."

"Anything else?"

"Ah yes! Another remarkable thing about this man is that he wore the stripes of a Group Captain. A rank that would be rather high for a regular pilot. And I remember thinking that he was rather young for a Group Captain..."

"Good, good... Fantastic! Now Victor, quick: think! What could this mean? Is there anything you can deduce from this? A very young chap with a very high rank?"

"Oh? Ah, yes! Wait, wait a minute... I would say an ADC... Yes, the ADC to a high ranking member of the General Air Staff..."

"An ADC! What's that? What's an ADC?"

"An aide-de-camp! The personal secretary of a Major-General or some such!"

"All right! Now we're getting somewhere..."

And then they had been cut off. But it didn't matter. Daisy would have liked to ask Victor if he had told inspector Cockett anything about this mystery man, but she already knew the answer: of course not, the whole story of this encounter had just occurred to him, and the inspector hadn't asked any questions anyway...

Sitting in the soft glow of the early-spring sun on her favourite bench near the Serpentine, Daisy thought back to that day. The excitement of the breakthrough; the relief at the idea that the crew and Victor himself were no longer suspects; how ecstatic she had felt! It was possible, after all, to find some useful information about what had happened to Ralph... But then, how did you act on it? What could you do? She would have liked to go back to the airbase at once and start pestering all and sundry about the mysterious visitor, but Major Mannings had made it quite clear that he would not allow her back at his station. She could have asked for Cedric's help once more, but he was likely to be back in Egypt by now, and his intervention probably wouldn't have changed the major's point of view. She could also have gotten in touch with Chief Inspector Cockett, but she didn't expect much support from that quarter either... And when you looked at it dispassionately, you had to admit there was very little to go on: how could you accuse this mysterious Group Captain of murder on such circumstantial evidence? Soon she had felt the benefits of her first big breakthrough turn to dust between her fingers.

She had kept in touch with Victor, who was as eager as she was to find out more, but as he had said: "I can't just go barging into the CO's office and demand information about that Group Captain... The major would throw me out on my ear!" Of course he had promised to keep his eyes peeled; he would make discreet inquiries left and right, but until now it had all been to no avail.

Then a few weeks ago she had heard from Victor that D-Daisy had been shot down. Most witnesses had declared that both her starboard engines had been on fire, but that it was impossible to say whether the crew had bailed out or not. Daisy assumed that they had, as long as the witnesses had seen her go down, but hadn't seen her exploding in one big ball of fire... You just had to hope that they had finally made their way to the Stalag Luft and a ticket for survival, bless their hearts.

And now, a few days ago, Daisy had finally phoned Chief Inspector Cockett in Great Dunmow. Even though the man was an awful pest, she had begged him for an interview. It had taken a lot of pleading and persuasion: she had played the card of the grieving widow aggressively, knowing full well that it was an argument the Chief Inspector was not totally immune to... So in the end he had relented. Tomorrow Daisy was taking an early train to Great Dunmow, but she was not looking forward to the interview.

Lost in thought while enjoying the glow of the sun, Daisy was brought back to the reality of Hyde Park by a hesitant male voice. "Excuse me Miss, I couldn't help noticing that you're blind... May I sit down on this bench?"

"Well, I don't own it, you know, so be seated, by all means... But I'd rather not talk, if you don't mind."

The man sat down next to her, mumbling a word of thanks, and kept quiet for a while. But of course, inevitably, this restraint didn't last. "Excuse me, but may I offer to be your guide when you leave the park?"

"Very kind of you, but no, thank you. There's no need. Hyde Park is utterly familiar to me, so I can manage just all right on my own..."

"Oh. I just wondered, you know..."

Daisy thought, "Please, not another saviour of damsels in distress, not another knight in shining armour... Not today, of all days!" Then, without saying a word, Daisy retrieved a handkerchief from her handbag, slowly took off her dark glasses, and turning her head slightly towards the man, she started polishing her glasses thoroughly, as if she needed them to be absolutely spotless. The man of course looked at her eyes, and gulped. Daisy was frowning fiercely, giving him her Gorgon stare. At the best of times her eyes were off-putting, but now, with the tear-duct infection she'd had—even though it had healed—her eyelids were still reddish, looking raw, and there were some last yellowish crusts clinging to them... Daisy heard the sound of receding footsteps: the man had quietly slipped away.

"It works every time," Daisy reflected. "Maybe I should simply take off my glasses when one of my perverts is lusting after me. That should put them off."

Once again the Chief Inspector was tapping with his pencil on his desk. "So... You wanted to see me. What can I do for you, Madam?"

To her dismay Daisy clearly heard that the man, once again, could hardly contain his merriment. "And I haven't even said a word yet," she thought. "What on earth does he think he's up to?" Suddenly it occurred to her that he might be merrily ogling her, just like that randy patient yesterday. Aloud she said, "Chief Inspector, I have some information that I'd like to share with you..."

"Oh, really? So you're still trying to solve the case on your own, eh?"

"No, no, not at all. I just happened to discuss some things with the crew... Surely you heard that they invited me to fly with them to Berlin? So we had many hours to discuss things..."

"All right. And what precious piece of information did you hear from them? Let's have it!"

"Well, maybe I'm going to tell you a lot of things that you already know, but here it is..." And Daisy explained the riddle of the Thermos flasks to the policeman, and told him about the mysterious Group Captain that Victor had encountered on the morning after Ralph's death. "So, Chief Inspector, to make a long story short, what I'm saying is: this man could possibly have been there to take away Ralph's Thermos, the murder weapon, but he was obviously not aware of the fact that there were *two* Thermoses... Does this make any sense to you?"

"Well, I can tell you one thing that doesn't make sense to me at all... First you say: 'Oh, I just happened to discuss these matters with the crew', then you tell me some wild theories that you concocted together with the batman... and you would still have me believe that you're not interfering with police work, and that you're not putting your pretty little nose into matters that are none of your business? Well, lady, allow me to laugh heartily at that! Har-har-har!"

"But, Chief Inspector, no matter what you say, the information I just gave you might be important. And for you it would be no trouble at all to ask Major Mannings about the identity of the Group Captain who was visiting the airbase on that day. Of course I have no idea how far you are with your investigation, but in the end we both want to get some results, don't we?"

"Funny that you should say that! As it happens, I have plenty of results, thank you very much..."

"So you've already found the culprit, then?"

"I'm not supposed to tell. For the time being the results of the police investigation are confidential."

"Well, am I not entitled to know a little more, if you happen to know who killed my husband? After all, when the case goes to court it will be public knowledge anyway..."

"Ah, but there's the rub, Madam. This case is not going to court."

"What? Why on earth not?"

"Again I'm not supposed to tell. But I'll make you an offer. You see, the only mystery I'm interested in, is *who* initiated the orders to pick up the case. I heard from the station commander that it was a certain Cedric Clifton who pulled an awful lot of weight to get you permission to snoop around at the airbase. The CO assured me that this Clifton chap was not a friend of his... Now, if you can tell me more about this, I'll tell you more about the results of the inquest..."

"Fair enough, Chief Inspector. I happen to know Cedric very well. He is a full cousin of my husband's, but it's his mother who is a Prendergast, and she's married to a Clifton, so Cedric and Ralph don't have the same family name... At any rate, when I found out about the poison in the Thermos, you know, from the pharmacist, Mr Dobbs... Well, when he heard about that, Cedric offered his help, and promised to

132

use his influence to get a coroner's inquest started. So yes, it *is* Cedric Clifton who was at the root of those orders you apparently received..."

"Well, I don't like being hounded! You do understand that, don't you, Mrs Prendergast?"

"Yes, yes, Chief Inspector, it won't happen again, I promise... Now for the results of that inquest you were talking about. Why did you say that the case is not going to court?"

"Well, as it happens, just a week ago I submitted my report to Coroner Jacobs of Saffron Walden, and the man has already read it, and reported back that he is very satisfied with my efficient handling of the case, and that he agrees wholeheartedly that we can let it rest. I have his letter here somewhere... So you see, I'm a happy man..."

"Yes, and what was the conclusion of the report, Chief Inspector?"

"In one word: accidental poisoning..."

"What? Accidental poisoning? Good God! And the coroner accepted that?"

"Oh yes, Mrs Prendergast. And mind you: it is not accidental death but accidental poisoning, which means that the poisoning has not been proven to be the cause of death... The Coroner accepted that conclusion too, and even congratulated me for making that very essential distinction..."

"But, for crying out loud, how can you say that? *Of course* the arsenic is the cause of death..."

"No-no-no, Mrs Prendergast. Have you actually seen the reports from Mr Dobbs and Doctor Westmore? I mean, of course you haven't, as you're blind, but are you aware of their contents?

"Yes, yes, of course, I had them read to me several times, and I have an excellent memory..."

"Well then, what I want to say is that it's all very inconclusive, you know. 'Traces of arsenic' in the coffee, 'but sample was watered down', and 'impossible to say if the coffee contained a lethal dose'. Then the doctor's report is even vaguer: 'small sample' and again 'traces of arsenic' and then 'a more thorough analysis would be needed'."

"Exactly, and that's the first thing that should have been done! Why didn't you order a full post-mortem?"

"Because the body was already buried good and well in West Sussex! There are limits to a policeman's authority, you know. At any rate, based on those reports, I had to conclude that the quantities of arsenic discovered were too small to be the cause of death. And of course that their source was most probably accidental. And my investigations at the RAF station have led me to the conclusion that all RAF personnel are completely above suspicion... I still believe, as I told you before, that your husband could very well have died from other causes. A heart attack, maybe, or a tiny piece of shrapnel that punctured a vital organ..."

"Good God, Chief Inspector, I can hear that you had great pleasure in writing your report. How convenient it must be to be able to just make the case for murder go away..."

"Don't you get fresh with me, young lady! Let's keep it nice..."

"Erm, of course... I only want to say this: the fact that the reports from Mr Dobbs and Doctor Westmore are inconclusive does not prove that arsenic was not the cause of death. This is particularly the case with arsenic, as small doses can accumulate in the body over time and kill by delayed action. Only a proper autopsy would tell us whether Ralph was poisoned or not... And if you want to argue the case for accidental poisoning: what was the source of the poison? And why was there only one victim? Why didn't it affect every coffee drinker or Thermos user at the base?"

"Whoa! Hold your horses! Take a deep breath, Mrs Prendergast. You are getting way above yourself, you know... There is no call for telling me how to do my job. I'm only being friendly, and I'm discussing my report with you as a courtesy. Now, your arguments are not entirely without merit, I have to admit it, but you have to look at this whole affair within a given perspective. For instance: what motive could anyone have had to murder a bomber pilot? Just let him do his job and let nature follow its course, so to speak…"

"Yes, all right, Chief Inspector, you have a valid point there… I have to admit that this aspect of the matter has me stumped: who on earth would want to kill my husband? But I have come to the conclusion that if someone wanted him dead, now would be the ideal moment to kill him. In the total chaos of the bombing campaign, it would be highly unlikely that anyone would even notice an arsenic poisoning… As to letting the nature of war follow its course, that is not as reliable as it looks on the surface. Some bomber crews survive against all odds… In particular, they can bail out and be taken prisoner by the enemy. My husband and his crew called it 'the only legitimate ticket to survive the war'. And as it happens, I just heard that *D for Daisy* was shot down, that her crew in all probability were able to bail out, and that perhaps they are now waiting for the end of the war in a German Stalag…"

"I'm quite sure, Madam, that I have no idea what you're talking about…"

"Well, the gist of it, Chief Inspector, is that the murderer might have been aware of these possibilities, and that he might not have wanted to take any chances."

"All right… Well, be that as it may, I still see no reason to change the conclusions of my report. And I may add that you should be grateful for those conclusions, Mrs Prendergast… You see, there is one more hypothesis that would have explained a lot, but that I did not want to mention in my report out of respect for the deceased, and that would be, to put it bluntly: suicide…"

"Suicide? No! That is *out of the question*, Chief Inspector, please!"

"Precisely. So do we agree on that matter, Madam, that it was not suicide?"

"Yes, yes, absolutely! I get your point, Sir..."

"And I would like to stress that there is another reason for you to be grateful: if it had turned out that your husband had indeed been murdered, you would have lost your war-widow allowance... Did you ever think of that, eh?"

"My war-widow allowance? Never mind that, Chief Inspector! Do you really think I care? I've just started working as a physical therapist: if need be I can take on more patients and make a living from it..."

"Good. Good for you, but I really think we're done, now. There's nothing more to discuss..."

"Well, I still believe that you should ask Major Mannings about that Group Captain... I have a mind to phone the CO myself..."

"Well, I would strongly advise against it, Mrs Prendergast. I will not tolerate any further interference from you... Do I make myself clear? A good day to you, Madam... May I still assume that you can find your own way out?"

"Yes, yes, no problem..."

Daisy stood up, gathered up her handbag and her cane and stepped over to the door. Then she turned around and faced the man still tapping with his pencil behind his desk. "You know what the problem is with you, really, Chief Inspector?"

"No! But I'm sure you're going to tell me..."

"You're a blundering fool!"

"Hey! Careful what you say, there. It could cost you dearly to insult a police officer!"

"Is that so? Well, sorry! Not funny! Blame the nerves!"

And Daisy slammed the door behind her as violently as she could. But as she stepped away she could clearly hear a burst of cackling laughter inside the Chief Inspector's office.

VI 1949: Five years later

It was a warm summer day. There was a knock at the front door of the flat in Tufnell Park, although Daisy was not expecting any visitors. Besides, most of her visitors just entered and called "Hello!" The door was never locked when Daisy was at home. So it was with a certain trepidation that she put on her dark glasses, walked over and opened the door, then discreetly sniffed the air for any familiar smells. There was definitely a man standing in front of her. Hesitantly Daisy said, "Cedric? Is that you?"

"You've got it in one!"

As Daisy stood frozen on the spot, her eyebrows raised high, Cedric asked, "May I come in? I have a little present for you..."

"Oh, sorry! Of course, *do* come in... You're the last person I was expecting, that's all..."

"Well, that's always nice to hear..."

"Take a seat... Can I get you something? You have a present for me?"

"Yes, a present, and a message..."

Presently Cedric pushed a little package into Daisy's hands. Then he sat down and watched Daisy unwrap it, still standing in the middle of the room. She unpacked a little cardboard box, opened it, and retrieved a little car. "A Dinky Toys car!" she exclaimed. "How on earth did you know that I *love* Dinky Toys?"

"Well, I didn't, actually… but you'll find out in a moment why I'm giving this to you."

"A sports car, how lovely!"

"Yes, the famous Morgan soft top two-seater…"

"Lovely, thank you. Would you like a beer? With this weather I like to drink a beer from time to time."

"Oh, yes, wonderful!"

While Daisy went to fetch two bottles from the fridge in the kitchen, Cedric took a good look around him in the front room of the flat. Then he called over to Daisy, "This place is almost empty; very Spartan!"

As Daisy returned from the kitchen she said, "Yes, that's probably because I'm blind. Why would you hang pictures on the walls if you cannot see them; why put rugs on the floor if it is only to trip over them; and why would you have many little pieces of furniture like most people seem to prefer, if it's only to bump into them?"

"Rational and well organized: that's our Daisy."

"Yes, and note how hollow the place sounds: I can practically hear the presence of the walls and aim straight for the doors! This may look like a poky little flat to you, Cedric, but it's the only place in the world where I'm completely at ease!"

"I see! Strange that I've never been here before, though, not even in Ralph's days…"

"Well, that's not so surprising, when you think how busy we all were with the war at the time."

"That's right… but I feel a bit ashamed that I didn't visit sooner *after* the war."

"Oh well, I suppose that by then we were all very busy picking up our own lives again… or what was left of them, at any rate."

"Yes, quite…"

They both sat in silence for a while and sipped from their beers. At length Daisy asked, "You said that you had a message for me?"

"Yes, indeed I have. It would sound something like this: dear Daisy, darling Daisy—depending for whom I'm speaking—, it's been exactly ten years since you came to Bottomleigh House and made our acquaintance for the very first time... That's why we would like to invite you to stay with us at the House again this summer, for a week or a couple of weeks. Let us renew our acquaintance and celebrate our old friendship. Signed: Margaret, Beatrice, Joan, William and yours truly."

"That sounds enticing... but are you certain that the others are aware of the fact that they are inviting me? I still meet up with Beatrice regularly, you know, and she told me nothing of this..."

"No, and she wasn't supposed to, but... Well, let me put it this way: it was *my* idea, yes, but the others are definitely coming, and they would be very disappointed indeed if you were not there. As a matter of fact, our little reunion wouldn't make much sense without you..."

"Hmm... Fair enough. But you do realise I have a job..."

"Yes, I heard about that from Beatrice. You're a 'physical therapist' now... But surely you don't really need to work, I mean, Ralph left you well provided for and you have a war-widow allowance?"

"Well, yes, but it is my pride and joy to be a working girl... At any rate, I'll have to ask for a leave of absence at the practice before I can accept your invitation."

"But surely they give you holidays, and it should not be a problem to take them in August... You see, I was planning to take you along with me to Bottomleigh House right now!"

"Oh, you mean: 'Dear Daisy, just pack your suitcase and come with me at once'?"

"Yes, precisely. You could telephone the practice from the House tomorrow morning to make the necessary arrangements. I'm sure it must be very quiet at the moment and that there should be no problem..."

"My dear Cedric, you're making an awful lot of assumptions... But you're lucky: there *is* very little to do at the practice right now, and I was just starting to feel rather bored by London in the August heat..."

"Capital! Go and pack your bag, then. Tell me if I can do anything to help..."

Half an hour later they came out of the block of flats and stepped on to the pavement, Cedric carrying Daisy's bag and she holding his arm. At the curb right in front of the building, a sports car was parked. Cedric explained, "I told you there was a reason why I gave you the Dinky Toys model. Well here it is: I'm taking you for a drive in the original, a Morgan sports car, rather low to the ground and not very roomy, as you will find out."

Indeed Daisy had to grope her way into the thing after Cedric had led her to the passenger side and opened the door for her. She lowered herself into a narrow and low-slung seat, and then she felt around her and sniffed the odour of brand-new, sun-baked upholstery. "What a good idea to offer me that miniature model, Cedric. Now at least I have an idea of what I'm sitting in..."

"Yes, and you'll find that there's nothing more pleasant than driving around in an open two-seater with the roof down on a hot day like this. That's why I recommended that you put on a headscarf."

Taking his place behind the wheel and turning the ignition key, Cedric made the engine roar, and they drove off. It took some time to drive through London, and he kept up an agreeable chatter during their ride: a running commentary on the monuments and the sights of the city centre as they drove past them. Daisy didn't say much. Then they reached the open countryside and speeded along the highway towards West Sussex. Over the noise of the engine and the wind in their ears Cedric cried, "How do you like it,

Daisy? Driving in the countryside in an open car?"

"Very nice! Almost as exciting as riding a bicycle, and as noisy as flying on a bomber! What's the idea with the sports car, anyway? It's brand new, isn't it?"

"Yes! Well, I've entered a new phase of my life, you know! So I felt like trying something different!"

"What's with the new phase? Are you getting married or something?"

"No, no. It's just, now that Ralph's father has passed away, I have become the Earl of Haverford and all that... you know?"

"Oh! I wasn't aware of that. So you became the heir to the title after Ralph died?"

"That's right! Didn't you know?"

"I wasn't quite aware of it, no. So in fact you've invited me to *your* house?"

"That's right! I'm the new master of Bottomleigh House, of course..."

"How strange: when Ralph was murdered, I racked my brains to find out *who* on earth could have a motive to kill him. And all the while the simple answer to that mystery was just staring in my face: the heir to his title! You, Cedric..."

"Dear God, Daisy, what a nasty thing to say! I mean, it is true, of course, but does that make me a suspect? I was in Egypt at the time of Ralph's death, remember?"

"Yes, yes. Of course. I was only reflecting, that's all..."

"And I helped you to get that inquest started, remember?"

"I know, I know. I'm being unfair, but you must forgive me... I'm in a rotten mood because I'm being periodically unwell. I'll try to put a zip-fastener on my lips..."

"Please... You do that!"

That evening at Bottomleigh House all six of them were sitting around the dining table, a much smaller table than in the old days. Cedric and William were wearing white ties; the ladies their formal evening dresses; Daisy looking quite lovely in the little black thing she had worn just once ten years ago, and which Cedric had asked her to take along when she was packing her bag. The host looked around the table approvingly and said, "Many things have changed since before the war..."

"You mean apart from the fact that we're wearing formal attire to dinner on a hot August night?"

"Yes, Cookie, if you'll just let me finish my sentence... I wanted to say that we no longer have any live-in staff at the House. As you can see, we are being served by the kitchen maid, with a little help from Cook... Everything very easy-going and informal, nowadays."

"Except for your own starched shirt-front, of course!"

"Cookie has a point, Cedric. Why the formal attire all of a sudden, if everything is supposed to be so easy-going?"

"Well, my dear Joan, I guess I need to compensate one thing by another. I'm trying to strike a balance, as it were."

"Speaking of which," Daisy said, "let's have a little survey of what has become of us all... Cedric we know, but how about you, Cookie... At the funeral I heard that you were living in America, and therefore you couldn't make it?"

"That's right, darling. I really regretted that I couldn't be there. I *adored* old Prendergast!"

Joan remarked, "We seem to meet up mainly at funerals, lately..."

"That's right," Cedric said. "And wouldn't it be a bit sad if we actually lapsed into one of those set-ups where you only see one another when someone dies... or gets married?"

Daisy said, "So, Cookie, you married an American?"

"Yes, *juste retour des choses*, isn't it? I met Mort in London in 1944, while he was working on Eisenhower's staff. He's a businessman now... It was love at first sight and all that: he doesn't mind my bubbly personality, he's even noisier than I am! We're a very American couple in that way... Though there *is* a funny twist to my story: for you lot I was always that uncouth half-American, but for all my new friends in Saint Louis, Missouri, I am the epitome of British sophistication!"

Everybody around the table had to laugh at that. Cedric said that Cookie's current visit to Britain was precisely the reason why the reunion had to take place now. In the meantime he kept pouring an excellent French wine into their glasses; that was another difference with ten years ago, when they had only been allowed water. Now Daisy asked William to tell what *he* was up to these days.

"I work at Manchester University; I'm one of the engineers on Alan Turing's computer project there. I worked with Turing during the war, of course, but I'm not allowed to tell..."

"Well, we already know that you lived at Bletchley Park and worked on an electric brain," Beatrice remarked.

"Good Lord! You lot are horrible! These are state secrets!"

"Come on, there are no state secrets at this table tonight. Tell us exactly what this hush-hush war project was..."

"Well, all right, but promise not to tell any further, I had to sign an oath of secrecy, you know... In short, we managed to crack the most secret German code, with a little help from a special computer, of course. And in the end we could read German encryption like an open book and the enemy couldn't keep any information hidden from us..."

"Well done!"

"Capital!"

"Britannia rules the waves!" they all cried jokingly. Cedric poured some more wine.

"Tell me, William," Daisy asked. "This computer you're working on, is it similar to what bomb-aimers used during the bombing campaign?"

"Oh no, my dear, not at all. A bomber *computor* is just an optical instrument that corrects its viewing angle according to the altitude and speed of the aircraft, so that the aimer can anticipate where his bombs will hit the ground..."

"And wind shear, don't forget wind shear..."

"Of course! At any rate, what we are creating with Turing is entirely different. It's an electric brain, like Beatrice said, which means it not only can calculate at high speed, but it can remember the figures, retrieve them at will and work on them according to instructions that are also stored in its memory... Anyway, I don't know if this makes any sense to you, or if you see the point of it, but I can assure you that it is a very exciting development. Alan Turing is a genius..."

"Never heard of him," Cookie interjected. "Is there any business potential in this thing?"

"I wouldn't know, but I think so, in the long run, yes."

"Am I allowed to tell my husband about it?"

"Oh yes. We publish our results: no secrets there..."

Presently Cedric said, "Shall we have some brandy? I'll ask the kitchen maid to bring the snifters..."

"Does this kitchen maid have a name?" Daisy asked.

"Mary, I believe. Why do you ask?"

"It used to be a tradition of this house to treat the servants like human beings... Remember how nice it was, when we performed our little sketch ten years ago, and the whole staff was there, and they laughed and applauded as enthusiastically as the masters and the guests..."

"Yes, take a snifter, Daisy, let us raise a toast to 'Murder of a corpse'... To the corpse!"

"To the corpse!" they all cried, even Daisy, though she found it rather in bad taste.

"Now we must hear from Joan and Beatrice what has become of them. Of course I already know about Beatrice myself, but Bee, you must tell us in your own words..."

"There's not much to tell, really. I'm not married, still living at home, waiting for Mister Right to come along and sweep me off my feet…"

"Oh come on, Bee, you're being too modest. You're awfully busy with different charities, one of which being to help a certain blind girl with all her mail and administrative chores. Beatrice has a good head for legal and financial matters… And then we have Joan left?"

"I'm living in Oxford now and I'm married to a don. I believe I'm the only one who has a baby…"

"Congratulations!" they cried. "We didn't know!"

"To the baby!" Cedric toasted.

Cookie remarked, "I bet that you could tell us an awful lot of juicy gossip about the goings-on at your hubby's college, couldn't you?"

"Maybe, but I'm no longer much interested, you know. I've settled, rather…"

"Hard to believe!"

Then Beatrice said, "And what about you, Daisy? Tell the others about your professional activity…"

"Well, I do believe that I'm the only working girl here. I'm a physical therapist and I work two and a half days a week at a group practice near St. Mary's Hospital. That's all…"

"Now it's you being too modest: you could tell us some gruesome stories about your work…"

"Yes, but I'd rather not even start on that, I could keep going forever… No, I'd rather conclude on a positive note: I think I have a wonderful job. Sometimes we get people who are in great pain, and often their doctors have no idea what to do about it. And when it turns out that we can actually *heal* them, that's always very gratifying…"

"And *I'm* very grateful to you that you're willing to take a few days off, dear Daisy. Remember that beer we had this afternoon? It seems a long while ago, already; we've had a lovely evening; I've had a bit too much to drink, and I think we should all go to bed... See you at breakfast tomorrow morning."

"Yes, Cedric. Let's all go bicycling tomorrow."

And for old times' sake, that's what they did. Daisy was delighted. "I haven't bicycled since the summer of forty-one, with Ralph. I haven't been able to do it since then: in London it's out of the question..."

"I'll never forget that first time," Cedric said, "suddenly you were chasing after Ralph at breakneck speed, shouting 'Tally-ho!'... We were mightily impressed!"

"Well, that's another thing that has changed. Ten years ago I was in very good shape because we did a lot of sports at school. But once you've left school, how much sports do you do? I try to do some gymnastics regularly, on the equipment we have at the group practice, but that's all..."

"In the RAF, at basic training, they made us run and march endlessly with heavy packs; tried to toughen us up... Does that sound familiar, William?"

"Not at all. In my case they skipped all that; I was a soldier in name only..."

"Lucky you!"

"That reminds me, Daisy: last night you seemed to know an awful lot of technical stuff about the bombing trade. I was impressed. Did you get that from Ralph?"

"No. Ralph told me a lot about his work, but he never bored me with technical details... But the thing is, I was taken along to Berlin on *D for Daisy* once... That's where I learned those details about bomb aiming. Believe me, dropping those bombs was the most gruesome experience of an operation that already had plenty of that!"

"Daisy! You flew to Berlin!" they cried. "Now we're *truly* impressed!"

"How *could* you?" Joan asked. "I would never have dared! Weren't you awfully afraid?"

"Of course I was! Right at the beginning I broke a couple of fingernails gripping the armrests of my collapsible seat, and that was only while we were taxiing to our starting position. When those aero-engines went roaring for take-off, I can tell you that I was shaking like a leaf!"

"But why did you do it? Had Ralph insisted?"

"No! I wasn't with Ralph: he would never have been allowed to take me with him... No, it was after Ralph was murdered, when Cedric managed to get me permission to visit Ralph's station."

"Were you suicidal, or something?" Cookie wanted to know.

"No, I took a calculated risk on a fact-finding mission."

"Do you still believe that Ralph was murdered?"

"You made a huge impression when you spoke up at Ralph's funeral and announced that he'd been poisoned..."

"Yes, well, I'm sorry about that, but I really had no choice..."

"And then, only a few months later, our parents and uncles and aunts told us that the results of the inquest had been published, and that it turned out that it was only an accident..."

"They told us: you see, poor Daisy was just being delusional!"

"We didn't necessarily believe them, of course."

"Well, that inquest was a complete sham, I can assure you. Ralph was murdered all right: my own investigation only confirmed that..."

"What did you find out?"

"Well, for one thing, a witness saw a suspicious person snooping around at the station only hours after Ralph's death. He was an RAF Group Captain, possibly an ADC to a very high ranking member of the General Air Staff..."

"Good Lord! And did you report that to the police?"

"Absolutely! But they were not interested. Believe me, I

met this Chief Inspector Cockett three times. He's the man who actually wrote the report for the inquest. I spoke with him at length. He is a very clever and lazy man, who knows exactly what his superiors want to hear. And they certainly don't want to hear that someone quite high within the RAF hierarchy might have murdered such a distinguished and gallant scion of England's landed gentry..."

"You mean Ralph..."

"Of course!"

"It's funny," Beatrice remarked. "At Ralph's funeral, you, Cedric, were wearing the stripes of a Group Captain, weren't you?"

"That's right, and I was indeed an ADC to a high ranking member of the General Air Staff in North Africa. So what about it? There were many of us in the same position, you know... Now I'm sorry to say this, even at the risk of making myself very unpopular, but isn't it just *possible* that the inquest is right and that you, Daisy, are biased by the fact that the victim was your husband?"

"There's always that possibility, of course, dear Cedric. But why would I believe this report when I know exactly which biases motivated it? It's *my* bias against *theirs*! Why should I not just think for myself and draw my own conclusions?"

At length they reached the hilltop where they had picnicked on their very first outing with Daisy, ten years back. Again they settled in the grass to eat their sandwiches, and those who could see it enjoyed the view. "At least here nothing has changed," Cedric remarked.

"Yes, this is lovely," they all agreed.

Presently Beatrice said, "To go back to what you were saying about your biases and theirs, Daisy: isn't it simply a matter of perception? Just like what Cookie told us last night?"

"I see what you mean: Cookie being half-American for

us, half-British for her American friends… But that tells us nothing about who Cookie really is. She's still a deep mystery to us all…"

"Darling!" Cookie cried, "that's the nicest compliment I've ever heard! I didn't come all the way across the ocean for nothing, then…"

"No, and we're delighted to have you… But what I want to say is this: in the case of Ralph's murder there is no mystery at all. Here we're dealing with an objective reality: he is dead! And I don't mind telling you that I'm sick and tired of hearing that I'm having delusions. No matter what the inquest report says, Ralph did not die of natural causes, and someone, somewhere, is responsible at some level. There's no such thing as *accidental* poisoning…"

"Eat your sandwich, darling," Cookie said. "You're making us very uncomfortable, banging on about this…"

"Well I'm awfully sorry, but I just have to get this off my chest, even at the risk of spoiling your appetite. After all, what are friends for? Now, try to put yourself in my place: my husband was murdered and he underwent very painful and protracted death throes. For several weeks, Ralph suffered acute torment from his bowels: stomach ache, diarrhoea and vomiting. That was the *physical* torture. But he couldn't go to the doctor because his symptoms looked too much like the symptoms of *fear*. So he had to keep his suffering to himself. That was the *mental* torture. One of the last words he said to the crew before he died was 'Sorry'. Ralph felt he had to apologise for making such a nuisance of himself… So yes, I'll keep saying that Ralph was murdered; and no, it's not a matter of perception… And now I'll stop banging on about it."

They ate in silence for a long while, no longer enjoying the food and the scenery that much, haunted by the picture that Daisy had just evoked in their minds. At length it was William who broke the silence: "Tell me something, Daisy.

What happened to Ralph's crew?"

"Oh, they are very well... They were shot down in forty-four, but they managed to bail out, were taken prisoners, and spent some time in a German Stalag. I meet up with some of them regularly, but one went back to Canada, another to Australia. All of them are still very grateful to me for lending my name to what turned out to be an exceptionally lucky kite. So you see: if he hadn't been murdered, Ralph would be sitting here with us right now."

"If I *have* to be fair to Cedric," Mrs Prendergast said, "I'll have to admit that he *did* ask me to stay on at Bottomleigh House. He even offered to overhaul part of the first floor so that I could have my own private quarters... But I couldn't bear to think of it... No. That I couldn't."

She took a sip of her tea from a very delicate china cup.

"Well, Aunty Stella," Beatrice said between two sips of her own, "we understand entirely how you must have felt!"

"Yes," Daisy added, "we were all very much shocked when we heard the news of Father's death..."

"Well, once again thank you all for coming to the funeral, and thank you two for your visit here today..."

"We hardly had a chance to talk properly at the funeral. These are such... *events*: very impersonal! So we're glad of the opportunity to visit you in your new home."

"Do you like it here, aunty? It seems cosy enough... I mean... cosy."

Beatrice looked around her as they were sitting in the front parlour of the little cottage. Daisy registered how very quiet the room was: a wall clock somewhere above her was slowly ticking.

"Yes, I guess it's nice, and I do like it here, but of course I would never have imagined my life like this: first my son gone, now my husband, and then the added distress, particular to our circles, of seeing your husband's title and properties go over into the hands of a very young man... I never liked that boy much; he never was my favourite... He didn't respect our values, you know, social justice and all that, what Gerald and I stood for in all those years."

"Oh, Aunty Stella, Cedric is all right, really. You have to take him as he is..."

"What strikes me," Daisy said, "is that he seems rather lonely. Maybe he would *really* have liked you to stay at the House, mother. Just to keep him company."

"Well, I would constantly have had the feeling that he was *gloating* over his good fortune. Knowing him the way I do, that's what I would expect..."

"Maybe Cedric should ask his own parents, I mean Uncle and Aunty Clifton, to come and live with him?"

"Undoubtedly they were also asked... But they have lives of their own, you know."

"Mother, do you mind if I inquire, but how old was Father when he passed away?"

"Well, darling, Gerald died too young, and I blame Ralph's death for that: he never recovered from our loss. But your father-in-law was no longer a young man either. He was seventy-two. You see, he took his sweet time to find me, then Maud came, who is now almost forty, then we had to wait a very long time for Ralph, and four years more for Margery. Why do you ask?"

"Oh, it just strikes me that, as you said, Cedric inherited the title and the deeds at a very young age... But anyway, how are my sisters? I haven't seen them since the funeral..."

"Well, for Maud nothing has changed, still married but childless, living with her surgeon husband in Southampton. As for Margery, my little girl, she's twenty-two now and studying chemistry at King's College in London. You must get in touch with her one of these days, Daisy, she's a great admirer of yours..."

"Really? And why's that?"

"Well, when she was twelve years old, of course, you were the wonderful sixteen-year-old blind girl who went bicycling! But nowadays it's because you are living on your own, darling, and because you're a working girl. Margery admires you enormously."

"All right, I'll keep that in mind. You must give me her address or a telephone number…"

When Daisy and Beatrice walked back from the cottage to Bottomleigh House, hand in hand, Daisy said, "I really feel sorry for Stella, you know."

"Yes, in the world of the gentry, a woman is fated to become a dowager and step aside for the new holder of the title."

"But what a difference it would have made if that had been Ralph!"

"Of course!"

"You know, Bee, I feel a bit ashamed that I neglected my in-laws so, after Ralph's death. I hardly ever came to see them, and now that Gerald is dead it's a bit too late. And they were so supportive of me and Ralph when we got married: they were absolutely wonderful. But of course after Ralph's death they resented me terribly for saying that he had been murdered…"

"Well, darling, during our whole visit with Stella you didn't use the word a single time. Not once."

"So you noticed! It's the least I can do: Stella just *clams up* when I say it…"

"Yes. And what you can't see is how she literally, physically *cringes*… Having said that, I believe I owe you an apology for that remark I made about 'perception' the other day. And you made a quite impressive speech there, and now I recognise that you're right: you *must* continue to say that Ralph was murdered. Absolutely…"

"Thanks, Bee. Apology accepted. And you know what else? I want you to give me a hug. A real one."

And on the footpath in the middle of a field the two young women stopped and held one another in a heartfelt embrace.

"Wasn't it fun to go shooting again?" Cedric offered. "I was amazed that you could still hold a pistol, compensate for recoil and shoot accurately enough..."

"Well, it's the same as riding a bicycle, isn't it? You never unlearn it... And I still have the same reservations about damaging my hearing. But you're right: it was fun to be back in that dusty old shooting range yesterday."

Cedric and Daisy were sitting face-to-face at a very fancy restaurant, just the two of them. Cedric had insisted on taking only Daisy out in his Morgan; the others were left in the able hands of Cook and her kitchen maid. He had driven down to Bognor Regis on the West Sussex coast, a pleasant enough trip in the open car, and on the Esplanade, on the sea front, they had parked near the Royal Hotel. There a table for two was reserved for them, but in the heat of the August evening the restaurant was rather stuffy. As soon as they were seated, Cedric described the place to Daisy quite enthusiastically: a glittering décor, fine crystal chandeliers hanging from abundantly stuccoed ceilings; gilded mirrors and richly framed oil paintings on the walls... Daisy shrugged and chuckled, "Do you realise, dear Cedric, that I have no way of picturing how gold or crystal glitters? But I get the idea of what you are trying to convey: for me it means hushed sounds, the softness of plush carpets under my feet, and the slightly musty smell that goes with the carpets..."

"You don't make it sound very appealing. All I can say is that since I was a child, this has always been my favourite place on the coast."

"Well *that* is a much more relevant piece of infor-mation... When *I* was a child we stayed at Brighton each summer, at *The Three Lions Family Pension*. We must have gone out eating at places just like this often enough."

"There you are then. Aren't those fond memories?"

"Yes, as long as it lasted... until boredom set in."

"And then what happened?"

"My dear father picked up on my change of mood immediately, and arranged for my first stay at Bottomleigh House."

"There you are then: we have a lot of memories in common."

Now a waiter stepped forward, presented a bottle to Cedric, and after the required ceremonial, poured some white wine for them. Daisy very cautiously started feeling her way around the clutter of cutlery and the platoon of glasses that crowded her place at the table. Cedric muttered, "This is the wine that goes with the oysters, dear, the outmost glass on your right..."

"Sorry... Ah, I've got it now. Is it all right to take a sip? I'm afraid I'm not very good at eating in fancy restaurants..."

"You're doing fine, Daisy. Just raise your glass and let us clink... You light up the whole place with your beauty, you know..."

"Well, thanks, but that's another thing I'm unable to picture. Funny, really: there was a time when Ralph also kept repeating how pretty, how beautiful, even how sexy I am... I told him to stop it. For a blind girl such compliments are very tiresome. Then Ralph started calling me 'my angel', but I said no: I'm not an angel either, and I don't want to be. Finally Ralph came up with 'my little wild flower' and *that* I found spot on. How do you like that for an endearment?"

"Oh yes: 'wild flower' suits you well..."

"Of course, when Ralph and I made love, there was no problem. He told me how soft my skin is and how firm my breasts, and those are compliments that I can fully understand... and appreciate."

"Daisy, please, keep your voice down a bit when you

discuss such a topic..."

"Are people at other tables eavesdropping?"

"No, not really, but you know... At any rate, to change the subject entirely, or maybe not: how do you picture the future, dear Daisy?"

"The future? I don't really think of it, I'm quite happy with my life. My colleagues all dream of starting their own practice, for instance, but I'm fully contented as a partner in a group practice; having a lot of colleagues is the whole point of working, in my opinion..."

"Yes, but how about children?"

"How about them indeed? I love to work with children, but I can never have children of my own, you know: it would be rather difficult for me to care for a little baby, and besides, a child of mine might be blind, which is all right by me, but would not necessarily make its father very happy..."

"Well, I've talked to a specialist in Harley Street, and he assured me that you are not more likely than any other woman to have a child with the rare birth defect that you have yourself..."

"Really? Well that's reassuring, certainly... but what a strange turn this conversation is taking."

"Well, yes. I suppose you're right. It is something I've had on my mind for a long time now, and I've decided that the moment has come to broach the subject. Hold your hand out, Daisy, I have another little present for you today..."

And saying this, Cedric whipped out a tiny, cube-like box and placed it delicately in the palm of Daisy's raised hand. "Open it," he said. Daisy did as she was told, and discovered that it was a jeweller's box containing a ring with some sort of faceted stone... She forced a smile on her face, but between her clenched teeth she hissed across the table, "Listen, Cedric, I'm sure people are watching us and I don't want to embarrass you in public, so I'll pretend to be delighted, but I can't accept this..."

155

"People are indeed watching us, Daisy, so just relax, just go along, put the confounded ring on your finger…"

When Daisy had done so, with a forced smile on her face that could be construed as full of delighted shyness, a few people at neighbouring tables clapped softly in their hands and muttered, "Lovely," "Congratulations," "How romantic."

In an impassioned tone of voice Cedric now declared, "Daisy Prendergast-Hayes, will you do me the great honour of becoming my wife?"

Without saying a word, Daisy picked up her handbag from the floor next to her chair, retrieved a handkerchief from its innards, slowly took off her dark glasses, and started polishing them thoroughly, as if she needed them to be absolutely spotless. Cedric hissed, "Daisy, what are you doing? You never show your eyes in public!"

Daisy kept smiling demonstratively, and hissed back, "I just want to make sure that people stop looking at me. And let's discuss your proposal later, shall we? On the way home for instance. For the moment we have a new dish to deal with."

And indeed, with a perfect sense of bad timing, a couple of waiters were crowding their table and serving the main course. Again Daisy was struggling with sprawling cutlery and spidery glasses. She almost upended her red wine, but just in the nick of time Cedric's hand shot forward and he managed to forestall Daisy's clumsy movement and prevent a mishap. "Careful, dear…"

"It's funny, you know," Daisy said in a normal and matter-of-fact tone of voice, "only yesterday, while you were away on 'business matters', William took me out in his Morris Minor to an inn on the River Arun. We lunched outside in the shade of a tree, sitting in a refreshing breeze on wooden benches, and then dear William also popped the question. He asked me to marry him…"

"God almighty!"

"Exactly! Ironic, isn't it? Of course dear William did *not* offer me a ring with a rock; he did *not* plan any babies on my behalf either, and at least he took the trouble to gather information about finding work as a therapist in Manchester. But still... well, I turned him down..."

"Of course!"

"Precisely... I told him exactly the same thing that I'm going to say to you: I have no intention of remarrying yet. I am still grieving the loss of my darling Ralph."

"But you've been a widow for more than five years now!"

"And I find it impossible to tell for how many years more I will be grieving... You know, neither of you would be happy with me, when it would turn out that I'm still thinking of Ralph all the time, every day... So I'm really doing you both a favour by turning you down."

"Well, I can only say that I wish *I* could inspire such devotion..."

After their dinner at the restaurant, once they were again ensconced in the low seats of the Morgan sports car, Daisy took off Cedric's diamond ring, slipped it back into its slot in the silk brocade lining of the jeweller's box, and handed it over to Cedric. "Here... as I said, I don't want this. No hard feelings I hope? I'm certain you can find some lovely young woman among your acquaintances who will be only too delighted to accept it..."

"Oh yes, there are more than enough of those, but I'm in love with none of them but you. I love you, Daisy, I always did, from the very first moment I set eyes on you..."

"No you didn't, Cedric. You only wanted to have what Ralph had. On that first day, ten years ago, you were pursuing Cookie, after she and Ralph had broken up. Then, when it transpired that Ralph had fallen in love with me, *that* is when you *too* fell in love with me... You were always obsessed by Ralph, Cedric. It is time for you to become your own man."

"Well, that *is* a harsh truth, Daisy."

"The truth always is..."

Cedric started the car and drove off with a roaring engine. Then, when they were driving on the highway and the level of noise had settled, he spoke again. "Dear Daisy, I'm afraid I must tell you some harsh truths of my own. You seem to think that you're very clever and that you don't need me or William..."

"Yes? Go on."

"Well, that's an illusion... You need other people, you know, and they're always kind to you because you're blind..."

"How nice of them."

"Just to give you an example: you're receiving a tidy little income from the assets that Ralph bequeathed to you. But you see, those assets were not his to give away, they should have gone to me. I could claim back that inheritance any time, I only need to pick up the phone and talk to my solicitors..."

"So what you're saying is that I'm living from charity... provided by you?"

"Well, that's the harsh truth, isn't it?"

"Maybe. But it was Ralph's wish to secure that income for me after his death. And Ralph was not only your cousin, he was also your friend. Now, if you choose to disregard your dead friend's will, and if this United Kingdom of ours chooses to keep applying laws that come straight from the Middle Ages, there's not much I can do about it. Call your solicitors any time you want, Cedric. I do have a profession, remember? If need be I can take on more patients and earn my own living, you know."

It was the last day of Daisy's stay. On Monday she was expected back at work. So for the last time that summer they went bicycling, and ended up on the hilltop where they liked to picnic. When they had finished eating their sandwiches and were still drinking some red wine out of light metal tumblers, Daisy suggested that they play a little game, "A blind people's game... hopefully amusing for you, but certainly very useful for me."

"You mean like the special pillow fight of old?"

"Precisely! But this time I want you to sit around me in a circle. You may take your wine with you. Maybe it will be even nicer if the gentlemen alternate with the ladies?"

The five friends shuffled around in the grass and settled in a circle, with Daisy making the sixth participant in the middle. "Now, if I understand it correctly, you normal people aren't really familiar with your own face. You only see it in the mirror in the morning, frontal view, left and right inverted... On the other hand, I am told, the faces of *others* are very familiar and meaningful to you indeed. That's why I want to ask each of you to give me a description of the person sitting to your right... After all, you lot know how *I* look, but I don't know how *any* of you looks, so after all these years, isn't it time to do something about it? Who wants to start?"

Cookie cried "I do! I'm sitting next to William... With him the first words that come to mind are 'boyish good looks'... But of course that's not something that you can picture in your mind..."

"That doesn't matter, darling, just tell me what you see and I'll sort it out for myself. We blind people just love words... 'Boyish' sounds... very nice, wouldn't you say?"

"Certainly. So boyish it is, but also very dark: almost black hair and dark, intelligent eyes... of course intelligent, but also with long dark lashes just like a girl's... This is great fun, actually."

"That's quite enough, Cookie-cutter! Now it's my turn and I will describe Joan. With her the operative words are 'English rose'... Long ginger blond hair, pink cheeks and light freckles all over the place; and beautiful green eyes. Joan could have been painted by the Pre-Raphaelites..."

"So am I correct to conclude that Joan is quite attractive after all? I always wondered."

"Oh yes, she's attractive all right..."

"And married, mister! Now it's my turn. This really *is* an amusing game... I'm sitting next to Beatrice, the very epitome of upper class womanhood. A tall figure; a noble profile; a characterful mouth; a Roman nose, and doe-like, soulful eyes..."

"There's no need to be so diplomatic about it, darling Joan. I'm rather bug-eyed and horsey, and Daisy knows that very well... Now it's my turn to describe Cedric. He's also tall and thin, but unlike me he has fair hair. In fact, his hair is so fair that it looks almost white. He has pale grey eyes; exceptionally pale, almost colourless. But in spite of that, or because of it, I would call him exceptionally good looking..."

"What's wrong, Cedric?" Cookie exclaimed. "You're looking a bit green around the gills!"

"Didn't you like my description of you?" Beatrice asked.

"Cedric is seeing a ghost," Daisy said. "I'm afraid this little game can sometimes play tricks with your sense of self."

"A ghost!" Cookie cried, "I just love ghost stories! Are blind people better at sensing the presence of spirits than we are, Daisy?"

"No, we can't see them at all, even when you normal people do... so we're immune, thank God! But there's one ghost that only Cedric would be able to see..." Now Daisy spoke in a low and spectral tone, inasmuch as her girl-like voice allowed: "I am referring to the ghost of Bottomleigh House, the ghost that appears to the new master, each time the title passes to another man... The ghost comes to check if the new master can pass muster..."

The others giggled, except for Cedric, who grumbled, "I don't find that funny at all, Daisy."

"No, you wouldn't, of course; sorry about that. Blame the nerves..."

VII   1945: V-E Day

Daisy had already known for more than four years that it was Cedric who had murdered Ralph. In fact, she could pinpoint precisely the day on which she had found this out. It had been on V-E Day, Tuesday the eighth of May 1945. Like many other people in Britain and in the world at large, she would never forget that day.

At 02:41 in the morning of the seventh—in fact in the middle of the night—at General Eisenhower's HQ at Reims, in the north of France, the Germans had signed an agreement of unconditional surrender to the Allies. This armistice was not meant to go into effect until the evening of the next day, but when the news had come out on the wireless that morning, all over London and elsewhere in Britain the people had started to rejoice straight away rather than wait for the eighth.

Mrs Maurois had come knocking at Daisy's door early that morning, telling her the news, urging her to put the wireless on, and they had listened together to the latest dispatches. The authorities announced that the next day, the eighth, would be a day off, an official day of celebration. "Well, all the same, Mrs Em, I do have to go to work now..." Before Daisy left, her old neighbour had hugged her tenderly, which didn't happen often.

On the way to work—on the tube—and all day long at

the practice, the wonderful news hung in the air and touched everything with a celebratory mood. Keeping up a conversation with the patients came effortlessly, the German surrender was the talk of the day.

When Daisy came back from work her neighbours were already celebrating. In Tufnell Park the whole neighbourhood had been out on the streets all day long. There were wireless sets turned on loud in the window openings so that the revellers could find out more about what was going on. People were hanging bunting and banners on the facades of their houses and between lampposts, they held fancy dress parades for the children, carried tables and chairs outside and held impromptu banquets... Choice supplies that had been set aside during many years of wartime rationing were brought out. It was a lovely, mellow, sunny day; people got drunk, laughed and shouted, sang and danced.

Daisy discovered a new side of her neighbours on that day. It was the first time since she lived there that Tufnell Park was no longer in the grip of the war. There was music on the wireless. People she hardly knew—acquaintances one greeted, known by voice only—offered her beer and things to eat, or invited her to dance. It took some time before she finally got home and could go to bed. She was exhausted.

The next day, the eighth of May, it just went on. In the morning Mrs Maurois came to fetch her blind neighbour and together, hand in hand, they roamed the streets and enjoyed the parties. But Daisy had something on her mind that kept the celebratory mood in check. "What is it, dear?" Mrs Maurois asked her in the end. "You don't seem to be enjoying yourself."

"Well, you know, I can't help thinking of Ralph..."

"Oh, of course, how silly of me! But you know, on a day like this, you just have to pretend that he is present too, somehow, somewhere... Just make believe that he is right here, next to you: what would you like to say to him?"

"I know exactly what I would like to say, but it would start me weeping to think of it, and then you know what happens..."

"Good grief, yes! I remember the horrible infection when that poor boy died... I'm so sorry!"

"Well, I don't know about you, Mrs Maurois, but I've had my fill of revelling... I think I'll go home now."

"Of course. I'll escort you."

Back in her flat, eating a sandwich for lunch, Daisy reflected on what her neighbour had said: what would you like to say to him? "Well, what I would like to ask you, darling Ralph, if *you* know the answer: Who on earth took you away from me?" Then she made herself a pot of tea, and while taking her first sips she thought back on the unresolved question of the Group Captain's identity. It was a bit more than a year since Chief Inspector Cockett had warned her not to pursue the matter... Surely she had let enough time go by, now? And with everybody celebrating in the streets, maybe it would be a good time to call her old acquaintance at Great Dunmow airbase. He would still be on duty there, but this time he was not going to say "Don't pester me, I have a bombing operation to run."

Daisy installed her phone on the coffee table and dialled the local switchboard operator, asking to be connected to Major Clarence Mannings, Commanding Officer of the RAF station at Great Dunmow. It took some time, the switchboard was busy, a lot of people all over Britain were phoning one another, but at length the connection was established.

"Major Mannings? Daisy Prendergast here. Do you remember me?"

"But of course, my dear Daisy! How could I forget you!"

"Have you heard the news?"

"Of course! The Germans have surrendered!"

He actually sounded glad to hear her voice. She congratulated him on their victory, and then without much ado, as they had only three minutes to talk, she managed to put to him quite innocently the question that was burning in her mind. She made sure not to use the word "murder", as that would surely drive him up the wall: "Who was this Group Captain that came to the base on the very morning after Ralph was killed?"

"Oh," the major answered lightly, "that was just Cedric Clifton, Air Vice-Marshal Rupert Clifton's boy. The same chap, by the way, who only a fortnight later pestered me to grant *you* access to my airbase. He really knows how to throw his weight around, that one..." Then he added, "You know, Daisy, I loved Ralph very much, almost like a son. I still deplore his death. What a tragedy!"

"Yes, indeed, Major. Thank you ever so much."

And that is how Daisy had learned the identity of the snooping Group Captain.

She was stunned and shocked. She leaned back in her armchair, feeling slightly dizzy, and almost nauseous with misery. A jumble of disjointed images and memories was spinning in her head, until she started thinking over and over, "Cedric! Good God, Cedric? How *could* you? Cedric..."

But the first flash of despair was immediately replaced by amazement. How was such a thing even possible? He had helped her! At the funeral he had volunteered his support at a moment when no one else was willing to even listen to her... Thinking back to the funeral, Daisy suddenly conjured up the memory of herself, taking an envelope out of her bag and handing it over to Cedric. "It would help tremendously if I could show that to the authorities concerned..."

Without further reflections, Daisy picked up the phone again and asked the switchboard operator to connect her to the office of the coroner in Saffron Walden. This was the man who had ordered the inquest about Ralph's death, and he had published the results after putting his signature under the report. "No recriminations, no wild accusations," Daisy admonished herself while she waited endlessly for the line to be connected.

When she finally had the man on the line and she had introduced herself, Daisy was relieved to hear that he too was in a very expansive mood, as she had hoped he would be... "Ah yes, Mrs Prendergast! I do remember who you are... To what do I owe the pleasure on this most memorable of all days?"

"Well, if you would be so kind as to allow me, there is something I would like to tell you regarding my husband's death..." And without giving the man enough time to groan or protest, Daisy started explaining the case of the two Thermos cans... only one accounted for... a Group Captain seen snooping on the premises on the very morning Ralph died... and then she put the question to him, "Now, my dear Mister Jacobs, if I told you that I have only recently learned the exact identity of this Group Captain, would you be interested at all? I mean to say: would you be willing to look into this matter?"

"Well, erm... Mrs Prendergast... I'm afraid not. Re-opening a case like this would be a very drastic step. Rather unprecedented, in fact. I would need to have a very good reason indeed to do so, but unfortunately, I have to tell you that your information is just too circumstantial, if you see what I mean..."

"Yes, I was afraid you would say that, Sir..."

Just at this moment they were interrupted by the voice of the switchboard operator muttering "Sorry, time's up..."

"Excuse me, Miss—operator? Coroner Jacobs speaking! This is important, please leave the line open! Now, where were we? Ah yes. I can assure you that I understand your frustration, Mrs Prendergast. It must be terrible, hearing that your husband did not die of natural causes... that is, in this case, enemy fire... and then it turns out that it *was* an accident, after all... I understand how you must have felt.

165

However..."

"Yes, yes, my dear Mister Jacobs, believe me, I have also come to the conclusion that I *must* accept the results of the inquest. But there is just one more question I would like to ask: when you ordered the inquest, a fortnight after Ralph's death, who asked you to do so?"

"Ah? Er, yes. I remember now. It was one Bernard Thistlehurst, a very young Senior Investigating Officer at Scotland Yard, one of the most brilliant criminal investigators of his generation. When a chap like that advises you to look more closely into an affair, you ignore his advice at your own peril..."

"Well, could you give me his number? Oh, and did he transmit the pharmacist's report to you? Mister Dobbs' report?"

"No. He did not. Chief Inspector Cockett already had that report..."

"Oh? Of course! The inspector got that from me... And the man's telephone number, please?"

And so this Bernard Thistlehurst of Scotland Yard was the next person Daisy got hold of on the telephone on V-E Day. It was funny to witness how these officials, the Major, the Coroner and the crack investigator at Scotland Yard, could not allow themselves to take the day off, but were delighted when a lady they hardly knew phoned them on this special day, at a moment when they had absolutely nothing to do. This man even turned out to be a great fan of Daisy's.

"When Cedric told me your story I was bowled over, my dear Daisy! May I call you Daisy? I mean, you're blind since birth, and *you* of all people found out that your husband's death was suspicious and that his coffee had been poisoned... I take a bow to you there, my dear!"

"So it was Cedric who came to you with my story?"

"Yes. We're old friends, you know. We went to school together... The Duke of Cumberland's Royal Military School

166

at Folkestone. Ever heard of it? That creates a bond, you know, something outsiders can't understand..."

"Then *you* brought the case to the attention of Coroner Jacobs in Saffron Walden?"

"That's right."

"And did Cedric give you... or show you, for that matter, the pharmacist's report about the poisoned coffee?"

"No. But I read that document when the coroner's report was published, of course..."

"But Cedric didn't give it to you on the day he came to see you about the case?"

"No, I'm positive he did not. Does it matter?"

"The thing is, he did have the original in his possession, because I gave it to him... Oh well, it's probably not important. I was just wondering, that's all... I shall not bother you any longer, Mister Thistlehurst."

"Please, Daisy, call me Bernard!"

"Well, my dear Bernard, goodbye. Thank you for your time."

As she sat next to her telephone in the front room of her flat, the sound of music and laughter drifting in from the street below, Daisy reflected on the three conversations she had just had. "It's the magic of this day... All of a sudden things are possible—even easy—that seamed unattainable only yesterday..."

Then she picked up the phone again and asked to be connected to her friend Beatrice's family residence. "Bee? It's Daisy! Would you like to come over to Tufnell Park? Great! And could you do something for me? I want you to bring along a photo of the gang... As recent a picture as you can find, I'll tell you why later..."

In fact, Daisy didn't want to tell her friend the real reason why she needed this photo; she didn't want her to be involved more than necessary. When Beatrice arrived, Daisy told her a vague story about her neighbour Mrs Maurois being curious about Ralph's background and about Bottomleigh House. Then, when she was handed the picture, she asked her friend to identify the sitters from left to right. It was Ralph on the left, then Cookie, Cedric, Beatrice herself, William, and Joan. Putting the photo away, Daisy invited Beatrice to go outside again and participate in the revelries.

It was only after her friend had left that Daisy took out the picture, put it in an envelope with a short note, and using a special writing frame to get the lines straight, she wrote Victor Hadley's address at Great Dunmow station on the front of it. She went out again and posted the letter in the nearest red box. Now that she had discovered the identity of the Group Captain, she needed to verify the testimony of her witness. Victor called the next day, as soon as he had received the photograph by the mail, and he assured Daisy that the man he had seen on the morning after Ralph died was the third person from the left. The first one was Ralph, the second one an unknown young lady, and the third one the man who had come to take a look at Ralph's room... "Yes, definitely, no doubt possible." So then Daisy had known that she had a positive identification.

The war still went on in Asia, against Japan, and for that reason it took some time before the soldiers were allowed to go home. The military bigwigs kept their options open to send British troops to the East. It lasted until the summer, when finally, on the fifteenth of August, the Japanese capitulated as well.

In the meantime the Americans had taken over London. They seemed to be everywhere. They had all the goodies: chocolate, cigarettes, nylon stockings... Daisy had a few US servicemen as patients, in need of physical therapy, who provided her with some of those goodies, and she was propositioned by a couple of them, but she turned them down.

168

Then finally the British soldiers were released from military service and life started to go back to a semblance of normality. Victor came to visit Daisy at her flat in Tufnell Park. It was the first time they met in person since that winter day at the end of forty-three, when Victor had been taken into custody by the police. "I can't tell you how much it meant to me, dear Daisy, that you never accused me, and did all you could to buck me up. I mean, *you* of all people, being the widow of the victim and all that, you stayed so calm and rational and... so *nice*, so *kind*!"

"Well, I'm glad I could make you feel better... And you see, now it turns out that Ralph's cousin did it!"

"Yes! When I think of that man, it makes my blood boil! Is there nothing we can do to get him arrested?"

"Apparently not. I've pestered that Chief Inspector, spoken to the coroner on the phone, even talked to a crack detective at Scotland Yard. They all made it clear that as long as we have so little hard evidence—for the moment we can only *infer* what happened—there is no way they are going to reopen the case... Besides, the crack detective is a childhood chum of Cedric's, so I had to be very careful about what I said to him."

"Now we still have to find out how Cedric administered the poison. Do you have anything new on that?"

"No, but I do have something that I want to show you... Just a minute."

Daisy stood up and retrieved Ralph's pocket diary from a shelf of her bookcase. "I'm sure this is very familiar to you, but that you have never looked inside..."

"Ralph's diary! That's right, I never did..."

"Well, I want you to go through it now and think back carefully. Somewhere in there, last week of October I think, there's a page with the name of another cousin, William, and his address at Bletchley Park in Buckinghamshire, and then Cedric's name and address in Cairo. And Ralph has written:

'send thank-you note'. Does it ring a bell? Now that I know that Cedric is the murderer, I have come to the conclusion that this might be important..."

Victor studied the tiny diary in silence for a while. "This brings back a lot of memories: the groceries I would go and buy for Ralph, and how careful he was to give me enough money and to keep correct accounts..."

"And how about that 'send thank-you note'?"

"Well obviously Ralph intended to send a note of thanks to his cousins... or at least to one of them... Wait a minute! Of course, the Arabian coffee! Ralph received a parcel from Bottomleigh, once, containing a pack of very special coffee that had been sent to him by a good friend... There was some Arab script on the wrapping and it was clearly something exclusive and exotic. So, for a couple of weeks, I prepared only this coffee for Ralph, and put it in his Thermos flasks as well... He never drank anything else until the pack was finished. That could be it!"

"Yes! And by the time you were through with this special coffee, of course, Ralph had ingested a deadly dose of arsenic. The coffee beans must have been laced with it, in a carefully measured way... And in the meantime Ralph probably did send that thank-you note to Cedric in Cairo, because he knew that it was Cedric who had sent him that delicious coffee from Egypt, by way of Bottomleigh House..."

"Yes... Yes, that is what must have happened!"

"Oh God! This is so frustrating! We're getting closer and closer to the solution. I wish I could call the inspector again and just goad that man into action!"

"Well, you just said there is no hope from that quarter."

"I know, but isn't there anything else we can do?"

"Well, do you have anything planned tonight? Do you have to work tomorrow?"

"Only in the afternoon. What do you have in mind?"

"I would like you to come with me. I want to show you

were *I* work."

"Well, I'd be delighted..."

Victor had a car and he drove them into the centre of London. "We're going to my place in the East End..."

"What kind of place?"

"Wait and see!"

After parking the car, Victor took Daisy's hand and led her into a tobacconist's shop. She recognized the smell of cheap, sweet cigars immediately, but at the same time there was something funny going on here. Normally a tobacconist's shop is a quiet place with a subdued atmosphere; here there was a lot of noise and excitement in the air. Several wireless sets were transmitting live reports of different horse- and dog-races, which made for a strange cacophony that didn't seem to disturb anyone. Daisy heard the voices of half a dozen customers, but instead of ordering cigarettes or cigars, they were placing bets with the man behind the counter. They all seemed to know her companion, crying, "Hey Victor! All right?" when they entered the shop. Victor greeted them back and seemed to know everyone by name.

"So the rumours were right: you're a bookmaker!"

"Yes, you've got it in one, Daisy."

"But isn't it illegal? What do you do when the police shows up?"

"There's a chap on the lookout in front of the shop who warns us. As soon as the cops arrive, the punters melt away through the back door, and the tobacconist just pretends that he's very fond of horse- and dog-races."

"But you're the one who runs the place?"

"That's right. Do you know that only recently I made a pile of money out of Churchill's defeat at the elections? Most people didn't see that coming, but I knew it all along!"

"I also voted for Labour..."

"Well, there you are! And the best part is, during the general elections I was still at the station in Great Dunmow, relaying my instructions in coded language and in three minute instalments!"

They walked through into a back office, and Victor led his guest to a comfortable armchair. "At this time of day I hold court here. I want you to listen without saying a word. Do you want something to drink? A beer perhaps?" Then very soon the first of many visitors was ushered in by the tobacconist. Each new visitor raised an eyebrow towards Victor when he saw Daisy sitting there in a corner of the office, and Victor nodded his head to indicate that they could speak freely in front of the blind lady. But the lady in question, of course, didn't perceive these silent exchanges.

For the next couple of hours a dozen visitors, all men, came in to discuss highly confidential matters with Ralph's former batman. Mainly about loans. Some wanted one, others couldn't pay back and made excuses, begged for an extension. Two men came in to discuss a turf dispute involving prostitutes; they appeared to be pimps and were seeking Victor's arbitration. There came a man who explained that he was looking for an extra supply of cocaine, because the Americans were clamouring for the stuff. Victor promised to keep an eye out, but told him that he didn't want to get involved directly. A moment later the same kind of conversation was repeated with another man, looking for a particular kind of firearm...

After a few hours of such consultations, Victor told the tobacconist that anyone who wanted to see him would have to come back the next evening. Then he took Daisy out to a club where they played excellent jazz, and they were led to a table in a far corner where they could talk in private. Victor ordered some drinks and snacks.

"Well, Victor" Daisy said after the first sip, "I must say that I'm impressed. I had no idea. You appear to be something of a kingpin in the London underworld!"

"Let's say just a pin, albeit a solid one, and only in my

own little backwater of the underworld. I hope you don't think less of me now..."

"Oh no! Who am I to judge? I'm a little surprised, that's all."

"For my defence I'd like to say this: if people want to take a bet, why should I object? They need some excitement in their lives... And if grown-up women want to offer themselves for money, and if men are willing to pay, let them be able to do so peaceably. If people want to forget themselves on illegal substances, again why should I object? They're doing no harm to anyone... In my view it's better if someone like me—with sound judgement—takes charge of all these matters, rather than some unscrupulous gangster."

"Of course, if you put it like that... But tell me something, Victor: did Chief Inspector Cockett know about this background of yours when he took you into custody?"

"Yes, and that is why he was so sure that he had found his murderer... In the end I almost started to believe it myself... because of my background!"

"Oh, poor thing! In the light of all this I realise now that your situation was even worse than I thought!"

"Well, you were so kind to me, Daisy—as I told you before—and tonight I think I wanted to show you who I really am, so that you may check your sympathy for me if you find you must..."

"No, that's not necessary at all... On the contrary: I find it even more remarkable that you, of all people, were such a devoted batman to those bomber pilots..."

"Oh, I was devoted all right: they were risking their lives every night, not me. Having said that, do you remember what we were discussing this afternoon? The frustration of finding out that this Cedric is the murderer, and that there is nothing we can do about it? Well, there is something I want to tell you just this once: if you want me to find someone to kill Cedric, you only need to say the word. It can be arranged…"

"Good Lord! That does sound tempting. But no… That wouldn't do at all!"

"Very well. Just let me know if you ever have a change of heart… In the meantime, we've got no choice but to pick up our lives and carry on… I myself have an interesting and rewarding life to go back to, as you can see, and I won't have too much trouble banishing this whole sorry affair from my mind… But for you it's different, of course, I realise that!"

"Well, I'll think it over, Victor. If one day I change my mind, I'll call you. You must give me your phone number…"

"I will. Just make sure to communicate in veiled terms on the telephone, that's all."

"Sure, and apart from all that, we must keep in touch anyway."

And keep in touch they did. In the early fall of that marvellous year, Ralph's crew finally resurfaced, repatriated out of German captivity. When they got in touch with her for a reunion, Daisy made sure that Victor was included in the invitation. The others agreed, seeing in the former batman a kind of stand-in for Ralph himself. And that is how they all got together one day, at Daisy's flat in Tufnell Park, in the fall of 1945.

To start with, they all toasted her: "To Daisy, our guardian angel!"

"Our faithful lodestar in times of trouble!"

"Our lucky charm!"

"And did I bring you guys any luck in your German prison camp?" Daisy asked.

"We'd rather not talk about that *now*," Sandy grumbled.

"Oh! come on, you chaps. You owe us a little debriefing here…"

"Well, for one thing, *Stalag Luft* is not at all what it is made out to be, you know," Ken started.

"We were quite all right at first, I suppose," Cray added, "But it all palled pretty fast."

"The German war machine was unravelling, and *who* do you suppose was at the receiving end of all the hardship, eh?"

"Pretty soon we were literally starving to death!"

"And then, just when our allies were going to liberate us, our guards started force-marching us to Nuremberg, the last Nazi stronghold or something..."

"And that was in the middle of the winter!"

"We starved; we froze to death!"

"So please, we don't want to talk about it anymore!"

Daisy said, "Have you noticed, dear Victor, how these chaps can tell such a gripping story collectively? Each one contributes only a snippet, but the whole makes perfect sense. That is something you can do only after hours and hours of practice on the intercom of a noisy bomber..."

"But to answer your question," Derek said, "yes, you did bring us luck in the end, dear Daisy, as we are all still alive and in one piece..."

"*D for Daisy* did turn out to be a truly lucky kite!"

"Though one thing that was also very important, of course," Ken remarked, "is that Ralph had the foresight to make us study German. That made all the difference in the world..."

"True," Derek said, "even when we were marching towards Nuremberg, there were old German women who would give us something to eat, sometimes... I mean, there are always kind people to be found everywhere, but it helps if you know their language a bit and if you can speak to them."

They were all enjoying their reunion tremendously, sitting close together on every available seat in the small flat, having a couple of beers. Apart from Victor, none of them had ever been in Ralph and Daisy's place before, and they remarked on that. Then Daisy said that she found it a pity that Rick, the new skipper, was not there.

"Oh! he was invited you know. He was with us during our debriefing at the station, when we were making our plans to come and visit you…"

"So why didn't he come?"

"We don't know. He didn't decline or anything, though he did seem to make rather non-committal noises…"

"You know," Daisy said, "after all this time I have only fond memories of our trip to Berlin, and Rick was very much part of that adventure."

"Of course! And we flew a dozen missions with him, and he was always an excellent skipper…"

"But there's nothing to be done if he doesn't want to join us."

Daisy felt a deep pang of sadness and regret at those words.

Finally the crew talked about their plans for the future. They all had pre-war trades to go back to, girlfriends and fiancées they now wanted to marry. Jerry Milton was looking forward to returning to Australia, and Derek was going back to Canada. "I have actually learned a new trade thanks to the war. I'm going to work in the Canadian aviation industry. I'm moving to Toronto to work for De Havilland there, as an engineer."

"Well," Daisy said, "I'm sure you'll be an outstanding aircraft builder. And always remember that you started small, with a balsa model of a Lancaster that had Dinky Toys wheels that could really turn round!"

"Ah! now that you mention it: I have the model with me. It's in the pocket of my coat, on the coat rack… I know that you positively adore that thing, so I wanted to give it to you as a farewell present."

"Oh Derek! Really? For keeps?"

"For keeps!"

Daisy flew into his arms and hugged him tenderly.

VIII   1950: The confrontation

Daisy was sitting at her kitchen table, quietly smoothing the facets of a plaster sculpture with a small rasp. The winter sunshine came in through the closed window, the sunrays warming her face just enough to be perceptible. Her fingers felt rough from the dry plaster dust, but the smooth edges she was working on were agreeable to the touch... On a couple of shelves on the wall near her, there were other little sculptures, Dinky Toys cars and aeroplanes, a miniature Eiffel Tower, and a balsa wood model of a Lancaster bomber.

Presently a man entered the kitchen, wearing a lady's dressing gown that was slightly too small for him. He stopped by Daisy's chair, bent over her from behind, put his arms around her shoulders and kissed her neck. "Good morning, lovely. Sorry that I fell asleep again... Not very polite of me."

"Don't worry, darling, you were tired, and for a good reason... And you see, I can amuse myself quite well."

"What is this? Supposed to be a work of art? You an artist now?"

"No, I wouldn't say that. Just having some fun."

"But it *is* abstract art!"

"Not for me. I call this 'Kitchen table'... I'm just trying to make a miniature model of a table as I perceive it."

"A table? It looks very strange for a table. I don't see any right angles or straight edges."

"That's my point exactly. My perception of angles is very vague, and when I follow the edge of a table with my fingers, it curves away from me left and right... The table top is smooth, but slightly wavy, don't ask me why... The only thing I perceive the same way as you, is that there are clear edges to a table top, so my little model has lots and lots of pronounced edges..."

"And it looks like something by Picasso... no offence."

"Ah yes, Picasso! Unfortunately, we blind people are not allowed to touch the sculptures in museums and galleries... But recently an artist friend of mine made a small copy of a Lipchitz for me. It's there on the upper shelve... And I must say that cubist sculpture makes a lot of sense to me..."

"Fascinating! And you sitting here so peacefully with your little rasps and gouges: that I find fascinating too... You were a real tiger in bed last night... and this morning!"

"You too, skipper," Daisy giggled, "you too!"

She put the plaster piece and her tools back on the shelf and started to sweep and mop the dust away from the table. "Let's have breakfast together, shall we? What can I fix you? Is eggs and bacon all right, and some coffee?"

"Yes, perfect. You know, sweetheart, I love it when you call me 'skipper'. It reminds me so of the good old days..."

"Yes, I also feel transported back in time in your company, and that's a very agreeable feeling... Here we are, reminiscing like two old crones... How old are you now by the way?"

"I'm twenty-eight, and you?"

"Twenty-seven! So you were, what, twenty-two or so when you took me along to Berlin that night?"

"Yep... And I was the oldest of the crew. They respected my seniority: Daddy knows best!"

"Oh, but you did impress us immensely with your maturity!"

"Maturity at twenty-two! The bloody war did that to you: they stole our youth from us... We were just a bunch of kids, operating the most deadly weapons in history.... and half of us paid for that with our lives. And then: not as much as a thank-you afterwards..."

"I know, I know... Here, butter your toast; the eggs and bacon will be ready in a jiffy!"

While they enjoyed their breakfast, they kept discussing the past, and the crew. "I see that you have Derek's cute little Lanc in your collection..."

"Yes. Actually, that funny little Lanc started me on my own sculpture projects..."

"And then I was missing Jerry Milton, our outstanding wireless, yesterday?"

"Yes, we haven't seen those two since '45, when they went back to Canada and Australia..."

"Well, you know, as a BOAC pilot I could arrange some rebates for them if we want to organise a real reunion one day..."

"Excellent idea, darling, we must keep that in mind... You know, I can't tell you how thrilled I was yesterday, when you finally showed up for one of our little gatherings... Why didn't you ever join us before?"

"Well, you know how it is: I was very busy, flying all over the world for British civil aviation. And besides, I always had the feeling that I was only the *new* skipper, and that I didn't really belong..."

"That, my dear Rick, is really silly! We were all absolutely thrilled to see you last night. And on *D for Daisy* at the time, the crew just adored you, I was a witness to that..."

"Well, I don't want to sound rancorous, but Ralph's presence was always quite dominating... To give you an example: when we were shot down and taken prisoners, it turned out that I was the *only* member of the crew who *didn't* speak any German! That is when I realised what kind of a leader Ralph had been... He was brilliant. It gave the crew tremendous self-confidence to know that if we had to bail out we would have every possible advantage on our side..."

"But darling, you were also very good at generating self-confidence: in the chaos above Berlin you stayed so calm, that was incredible!"

"Thanks, Daisy. At any rate, how the others pleaded with the mob! Those German villagers would have slaughtered us right there if it hadn't been for the fact that the whole crew could speak the language!"

"Well, if it can be any consolation to you: even *I* was jealous of the crew and felt inadequate, sometimes... But on the other hand, they all keep Ralph's memory alive in a way that no one else can..."

"Yes, I get that... and what I found very touching is that even our old batman has joined the club..."

"Victor! Oh yes, the most loyal supporter of all! And do you realise that he is something of a kingpin in the London underworld? Of course he didn't mention it last night, but if you're looking for something special, a Chinese mistress, an exotic narcotic or forbidden weaponry, Victor is your man!"

"Well-well! And I thought he had always been a butler, and would go back to being a 'gentleman's gentleman'..."

They were silent for a while, enjoying one another's company while they were eating. Then Richard Clayton took Daisy's hand and said, "Dear Daisy... I do hope this is not meant to be a one-off?"

"Oh no, of course not! The only thing is... I'm still very much involved with Ralph, if you know what I mean, and I wouldn't want to make you feel like a second fiddle or something... But having said that, I do like the idea of an intercontinental pilot with a girl in each port of call, and that I should become your girl in London..."

"That sounds good to me; I'll take you up on that. And maybe I can take you along on a flight, sometime. I started my career on South American Airways, before we were incorporated into BOAC, and I still fly to Rio on a regular basis. Would you like to visit Rio one day?"

"Oh yes! Do they sell models of the Sugarloaf Mountain as a souvenir?"

"Certainly! I'll take you to the top on the cable car and buy you a model right on the spot..."

"Wonderful! You know, with Bee, a friend of mine, we actually climbed the Eiffel Tower: we took the stairs!"

"Well, there you are then. We'll make a real world traveller out of you!"

As soon as Rick had washed and dressed, Daisy asked him to go downstairs and pick up her mail for her in the lobby. "I'm expecting some news from my solicitors..."

When he came back there was indeed a solid brown envelope among the letters, with the name of a well-known solicitor's firm printed on it. "Aren't the services of such a firm rather expensive?"

"It's my father who pays their bills. He's a banker and he can afford it. And he assures me they are the best..."

"And why does my sweet Daisy need the services of such excellent solicitors?"

"Well, it's because of a cousin of Ralph's, who inherited the title after my father-in-law died. This cousin is trying to contest Ralph's will and claims that *he* should have inherited everything Ralph left to *me*... My father was furious on my behalf, of course, and insisted I should hire good solicitors and fight for my rights. What you have there is their monthly report. You must open it and read it to me..."

"Well darling, I'll be honoured..."

While Rick opened the envelope, Daisy explained, "My solicitors have argued that the properties Ralph possessed

181

before his father's death are not part of the deeds that Cedric, the cousin, is entitled to *after* the old earl died..."

"Sounds complicated... Let's see... Ah, here it is!" Rick started reading the report aloud. It appeared that Cedric's solicitors were now arguing that the flat in Tufnell Park was part of the residences of the Earl of Haverford. That in a spirit of conciliation, the Earl was willing to drop his prior claim, if in exchange Daisy would be willing to relinquish this modest property...

"What!" Daisy cried, "now he wants to evict me from my flat!"

"Wait a minute, there is more..." The solicitors recommended that she accept the proposal. For one thing, the Justice of the Peace was bound to be very receptive to this offer of conciliation, and on the other hand, one could argue that the flat was of very little value compared to the sum total of the deeds bequeathed by Ralph...

"Yes, but I *live* here; this is my *home*, for Pete's sake!"

Rick finished reading the letter, "The case has to be submitted to the Justice of the Peace before the end of March, so therefore, dear Madam, we would appreciate if you could communicate your decision to us before the end of the month..."

"What day are we, anyway?"

"It's the sixteenth of January..."

"Hmm, not much time left to think it over, then... Anything else?"

"No, that's it... I'm awfully sorry to be the one who has to bring such bad tidings..."

"It's all right, darling... So the first claim was just a smoke screen all along: they didn't stand a chance with that at any rate. And now Cedric wants to take away my flat only to annoy me... How clever and dishonest these people are! You know, sometimes I wonder why we fought the war... The Germans were the bad guys and we were supposed to be

good and decent. Well, in my experience there is no differ-
rence at all!"

"My poor Daisy, it seems to me that you've made a very
hard landing into the real world."

It was two o'clock in the morning on a cold winter night.
Daisy walked up the driveway to Bottomleigh House in the
pitch darkness. According to her information there would be
no moon, and probably a cloudy sky. But to her it made no
difference at all: the path was utterly familiar; it could have
been bright daylight; she navigated confidently on her
memory of untold strolls with Ralph up and down this lane.
When she neared the house she could perceive it's presence
by the echoes of her steps on the gravel. Then, instead of
turning to the right, where the porch and the front door were
situated, she turned to the left, walked stealthily in the
direction of the garages, turned around the corner of the
building and counted her steps along the basement
windows, at the foot of the terrace wall. Presently she
stopped, put on a pair of fine lady's wrist gloves, and then
she stooped, groped for the fourth window, felt the doctored
latch give way as it should... Some things never change in
old houses. She opened the basement window noiselessly.

Now she was inside the house, in the basement. She
easily found the boiler room, the main valve, and she turned
the boiler down a notch or two. Nothing outlandish, just
enough to let the temperature drop a little. Then she went
upstairs. During the next half hour Daisy took stock of
Bottomleigh House. She checked every room except Cedric's
bedroom and verified that there was no one else on the
premises. She moved around swiftly: after all these years she
had the place mapped in her mind, utterly familiar, for her it
was like walking those corridors in bright daylight.

She needed to make some preparations; execute a
carefully thought out plan. In the hall on the ground floor, at

the back of the stairs, there was a small box, where you could disconnect all the phones of the House from the outside world. Daisy did so. "Remember to reconnect afterwards," she admonished herself. Then she went into Mr Prendergast's old study. Cedric used it as his office nowadays, but the creaky wooden floor was still the same: excellent. Daisy went over to the French windows that opened onto the corner of the terrace at the back of the House; she opened one of them and left it ajar, so as to let some cold air enter from outside.

Now for a more complicated matter. She climbed on a chair she had set exactly in the middle of the room, reached up for the ceiling and found the light fixture, disengaged the bayonet pins of the bulbs inside and removed them. Then she did the same for the desk lamp and a standing lamp in the corner. She stowed the bulbs away in her handbag. There was a weapons display cabinet against the wall next to the desk. Daisy knew where to find the key in the drawer of the desk, and having retrieved it, she opened the glass doors of the cabinet. She groped among the guns and pistols on display until she found a particular pistol, a Luger. She took it out, extracted the magazine, emptied it into her handbag and inserted another set of bullets; she put the Luger back, but left the glass door ajar, the key still in the lock. Before she left the office, she made sure that the door key was there too, on the inside.

Daisy now went back to the hall and switched on the lights there, then those in the little corridor leading to the office. She did the same with the lights on the stairs and on the landing upstairs. Of course she had no way of knowing that those lights were on, other than toggling each brass switch and hearing it click just once. Finally she was standing in front of Cedric's bedroom door. She opened it as silently as she could, opened it just wide enough to slip inside without allowing too much light from the landing to enter the room. As expected, Cedric's quilted silk dressing gown was hanging heavily on a peg on the inside of the door. At this time of the year, with the heating turned down a notch and the open windows letting in some cold air, he would certainly not leave his bedroom without putting it on... Excellent.

Presently Daisy stood for a long while close to Cedric's bed, listening to the shallow breathing of someone sleeping deeply. She listened carefully, sniffed the air, making sure that there was no one else in the bed: no lady guest sleeping here tonight... "Just *his* breathing... and mine." She went over to the window, pulled the curtains aside a bit and opened the window a crack, letting in some cold air from outside. She waited for a while, allowing the temperature in the room to go down just a little "My poor Cedric," she reflected, "how lonely you are in this big house..."

Now Daisy bent over by the bed and softly touched Cedric's shoulder. "Wakey-wakey, lazybones, it's almost three in the morning," she said softly. She could hear from the way his breathing faltered that Cedric was waking up. Then he mumbled groggily, "What is it? Who's there?" But before he had the time to clear his mind, Daisy silently stepped away from the bed and slipped out of the room, leaving the door almost closed, so that only a slit of light from the landing shone through.

When a moment later Cedric appeared on the threshold of his room, his eyes blinking in the light, Daisy was just disappearing at the foot of the stairs. Then, when he started walking down, she slipped back into the office at the end of the corridor on the ground floor. Cedric followed the lights and the glimpse he'd caught of a female figure disappearing out of sight. Then he opened the door of his study tentatively, groped for the switch with one hand while still holding on to the door with the other. He heard the clicking of the light switch, but nothing happened: the room remained dark.

"Step inside, Cedric!" a voice commanded.

"Daisy! What on earth are *you* doing here?"

Cedric opened the door wider, and in the light coming from the corridor, he could just make out the outline of a familiar presence sitting in an armchair at the back of the room. Immediately he stepped over to his desk and lifted the receiver from the telephone standing there. "I'm calling the police at once! This is trespassing; you have broken into my house!" But he hardly had the time to find out that the line was dead, before Daisy sprang to the door, closed it, turned the key, and pocketed that. The room was plunged into darkness. "Hey! What's the idea?"

"Sit down, Cedric! We need to talk…"

"But I don't want to sit in the dark!"

"Well, for just this once I want to have that advantage over you. Because I may be blind, you understand, but right now *I* am *not* sitting in the dark… I want to talk about Ralph's murder."

"Oh no, not that again!"

"Yes. You're going to listen to me. And don't get any funny ideas in your head… First, this room has a conveniently creaky floor, as you well know, and I can hear every movement you make. Secondly, I have a pistol in my hand. It is taped to my wrist so that if you try to wrestle it from me I can shoot you first; and you know from experience that I can shoot well enough…"

"All right, all right, let's get on with this charade. What do you want from me?"

"I just want to tell you a story… It goes like this: on V-E Day, in forty-five, when everybody was celebrating in the streets, I decided that it would be a good time to call my old friend Major Mannings at Great Dunmow airbase. When I got him on the phone, I asked him as innocently as I could: who *was* this Group Captain that came to the base on the very morning after Ralph died? 'Oh,' the major answered, 'that was just Cedric Clifton, Air Vice-Marshal Rupert Clifton's boy...' And that's how I learned the identity of the snooping Group Captain. So you lied when you told me that you flew over from Cairo 'as soon as you heard the news'. You were already in Britain, and probably in a position to monitor the lists of RAF casualties as soon as they came in at headquarters. You wanted to make sure you could go and recuperate the Thermos that had contained the coffee that *you* had laced with poison. Only, there were *two* Thermoses."

"What are you talking about? All this is just idle speculation! May I remind you that *I* was the one who got you permission to investigate at the airbase? It was *I*, remember, who asked Doctor Westmore to take samples... How do you reconcile your accusations with that, eh?"

"It was a tactical move on your part, and it worked brilliantly. I must say I'm impressed by how you kept your cool at Ralph's funeral... The moment you found out that you had blundered with that Thermos, you decided that it would be better, no matter the consequences, to be seen to help me find the culprit, precisely because it was you."

"You can't prove any of this, can you? I just did the decent thing..."

"Well, whatever you say... But the story goes further. On V-E Day I also managed to get hold of the coroner in Saffron Walden, the man who ordered the inquest. Again we talked amiably, and I managed to cajole him into giving me the name of an old school friend of yours at Scotland Yard. This, of course, being the man who had initiated the inquest on your behalf..."

"There you are, I did everything in my power to help..."

"Yes, but the interesting thing, you see, is that both men assured me that they *did not* receive the pharmacist's report from you. Of course Chief Inspector Cockett already had it, but *you* didn't know that. So it *is* a bit suspicious, isn't it, that you didn't even show it to your friend at the Yard? I remember you saying at the funeral that it would help tremendously if you could show that letter to the authorities concerned..."

"Well, it wasn't even necessary to show it to old Thistlehurst, he offered his assistance right away, and the result of my efforts proves that I was really trying to help..."

"But I still believe you were only interested in suppressing evidence when you asked me to give you that letter... At any rate, after that, I showed a photograph of the gang to my witness, Ralph's batman, and he confirmed that you were on it. So then I had a positive identification. It is of course quite tragic that because I'm blind, I have no way of telling how *anyone* looks. Otherwise I would have known it was you the moment Victor gave me a description of you at first..."

"So that little game you had us play on the last day of your stay, last summer... You in fact already *knew* what I look like, then?"

"Yes. And *you* have just implicitly admitted that you *are* the snooping Group Captain."

"I did no such thing! I can only deny it and protest my innocence... And you have no real evidence against me anyway... So may I ask if you intend to go on for long with this? I'm starting to find all these explanations very long-winded and tiresome. I'd like to go back to bed..."

"Well that's tough, because there's more to come, and you are going to listen patiently like a good boy. Now, the last piece of the puzzle that needed to be solved, of course, was: how on earth did the murderer—whoever he is—manage to administer a lethal dose of arsenic to his victim? It is Victor who found the solution, when I showed him Ralph's pocket diary. There's a page with William's name, and his address at Bletchley Park, and your name and address in Cairo. And Ralph has added: 'send thank-you note' When he saw this, Victor suddenly remembered that Ralph had once received by post a packet of very special coffee. There was some Arab script on the label and it was clearly something exclusive and exotic. So, for a couple of weeks, Victor prepared this coffee for his officer to take along on operations, and Ralph never drank anything else until the packet was finished. And by then, of course, he had ingested a deadly dose of arsenic... And in the meantime Ralph probably sent that thank-you note to your address in Cairo, because he knew that it was *you* who had sent him that delicious coffee from Egypt. Whether you were still there to receive the note or not, I cannot tell. As for your address—and William's—Ralph must have been in touch with his uncle Rupert, your Dad, and gotten the information from him. And that is the last piece of the puzzle; it fits just so, and completes the picture of your crime..."

"Gosh, Daisy, you know... I was in love with you for many years and it really pains me that you should think I'm capable of such heinous villainy!"

"Well, all I can say is that there's no doubt whatsoever in my mind that you are. You always had a ruthless and reckless streak, did you not, Cedric? I only need to think back to the episode of the pig that you shot with a dumdum bullet... It makes one shudder and it gives one a horrifying insight into the workings of a mind like yours... And what I really find galling about this whole plot, by the way, is that all along you must have had a nice safe job as an ADC to some chum of your father's. Your own life was never at risk, was it, Cedric?"

"So what if it wasn't? Ralph actually volunteered for a bloody dangerous position. He didn't have to. He could have done just like me, and Dad would have arranged a cushy job for him as well..."

"Precisely! And instead of despising him, you should admire him all the more for not doing that, you coward! Come to think of it: you were also jealous of Ralph's complete

189

lack of cowardice, probably… And let us not forget, please, that if you hadn't murdered him, Ralph would still be alive! He accepted the risks he had to, but he didn't wish to die, you know."

"Well, fine. But you have absolutely no proof for any of the allegations you are levelling at me. And I would strongly suggest that you keep those allegations—and your poor opinion of me—to yourself, or else you will be liable to prosecution for slander!"

"Oh, don't worry, Cedric, this conversation will never again be mentioned or alluded to outside this room. But beware of what you may set in motion when you resort to legal action, that is all I can say… For one thing, if you hadn't started pestering me by way of your solicitors, we would not be having this conversation."

"Fine! Can I go back to bed now?"

"No. You certainly cannot. I'm not finished with the story I want to tell. So, in the summer of forty-five, just after Victor was demobbed, we had effectively solved the case of Ralph's murder. It was absolutely clear in our minds that we had identified the killer. Only now the question was: what could we do with that information? I showed Victor my copy of the coroner's inquest, and he agreed with me that it did not look good for us. After all, we had very little hard evidence; we could only *infer* what had happened. So in the end, after many discussions, we decided to just forget it and get on with our lives… And I tried, Cedric, I tried very hard to let it rest, to get it out of my mind, but I can assure you that it's the most difficult thing in the world… How can you force yourself to forget a thing like that? And then, after four years, *you* turn up on my doorstep and invite me to a house party at Bottomleigh. Which, it turns out, now belongs to you! What happened last summer I also found really galling… Not only do you think you can get away with murder, but you even start pestering your victim's widow into marrying you!"

Cedric chuckled. "So my suit and my proposal *did* make an impression, after all!"

"Well, as it turns out it actually helped me, in a way. Unwittingly you managed to push me into the arms of another man... For the first time since Ralph died I think I am falling in love again..."

"Well, bully for you!"

"But there is another thing that has sustained me in all those years, and also during my visit here last summer. You see, after obsessing endlessly over what had happened, suddenly I stumbled on an astonishing truth: if *you* managed to get away with murder, it is only because *I* am blind—and a woman—and so no one ever listens to me. But this fact, I then realized, can also work to my advantage. It could work the other way round. I myself could also get away with murder for the very same reason! If I kill *you*, who will ever suspect a poor blind woman like me?"

"I beg your pardon? Are you telling me that you want to kill me?"

"Not so fast! I'm only telling you what has sustained me all those years. The dream that provided me with the strength to pull through. When you turned up on my doorstep last summer, I could have kicked you out and yelled at you in a very unladylike manner... But I managed to keep my cool and decided on the spot to go along with your little fantasies. I came with you to this house on a spying mission. And that is how I identified this office, where we are sitting now, as the ideal location for a tribunal..."

"Again, I beg your pardon? I'm starting to find your charade in very bad taste, Daisy. Lifting people out of their beds in the middle of the night and sequestrating them in pitch darkness; and now you start to threaten me?"

"I know it's not ideal. One is not supposed to be judge and jury at the same time. And certainly not executioner as well, but there it is... We've heard the witnesses' declarations and sifted through all the evidence, and now the accused is declared guilty as charged."

"Wait a minute! You're crazy! Listen very carefully, Daisy. I have no doubt that you could shoot your pistol effectively enough to kill me..."

"Thank you for teaching me so well..."

"But blind or not, you will not get away with it. I can assure you that if you kill me you will be hanged in the end."

"My-my, all of a sudden we have great confidence in the police and the justice system, haven't we? But let me tell you what is going to happen. Tomorrow morning one of your staff members, and later the local police, will find you dead on the office floor, gripping your prized Luger in your right hand, and one of your beloved dumdum bullets will have exploded in your chest... They will find other dumdum bullets in the Luger's magazine. In fact, I have already put them there..."

All of a sudden Cedric stood up, jumped up so abruptly, that he overturned his office chair, which clattered loudly on the wooden floor. Daisy could hear his steps as he fled and pressed himself in the farthest corner of the room and stayed there, breathing hard. She carried on with her speech undisturbed.

"The police will be very embarrassed, as it would not do at all to tell the populace that the Earl of Haverford has committed suicide. Because that is what it will look like to them. So they will close their eyes and pinch their noses and leave the crime scene as fast as they can, then they will flee to their office at the local police station and immediately start writing a beautiful report to the effect that the squire died in a tragic accident. While fondling his beloved collection of firearms, he did not take into account the fact that the safety latch of his Luger was not secured and that the weapon was loaded with *special* ammunition... I don't know the local police, but I'm sure they know *you* very well. They will know how lonely and depressed you have been lately. They will draw the obvious conclusions and do the right thing by you..."

"You crazy bitch! You want to shoot me with my own Luger, with a dumdum bullet? It will never work! You're blind! You're not *that* good!"

Suddenly Cedric lurched again, and Daisy thought that he might be coming for her, but she heard him moving sideways, bumping into the desk, then groping for the weapons cabinet. Daisy heard the clatter of the glass doors as he bumped into the cabinet. In the lower part of it there were drawers, in which Cedric started to rummage.

"What are you doing?" Daisy asked. "You're making me nervous. Please sit down..."

"Aha!" Cedric exclaimed. "A flashlight! I knew it must be there."

The hinges of the glass doors squeaked as he opened them. "The Luger is still there after all," he muttered. Then with a few steps he changed his position again.

"My dear Daisy, do you realise that by now I am crouching behind my desk? Do you still believe you can shoot me?"

"If you are referring to that flimsy Louis XVI card table with the inlaid mother-of-pearl shepherd and shepherdess, then the answer is yes."

"Well, I've got my Luger aimed at you, Daisy, and I have a flashlight in my other hand, so I will kill you if I must!"

"Very well, Cedric. Now, if you would care to shine your flashlight on my hands, you will find out that I don't have a pistol after all. But can you see what I'm holding in my right hand instead?"

"Erm... a cigarette case?"

"That's right! Don't you recognise it? Take a good look: don't you remember William's device? The remotely controlled radio transmitter? That is what I'm holding in my hand right now. All this time I've had my thumb resting lightly on the push-button, ready to send a signal if you tried anything clever... Of course, there is also a receiver, if you recall, and it still works splendidly after all these years. But recently it has been modified by an Irish bomb expert; a man Victor recruited for me; in fact a so-called terrorist... You see, the receiver, located in its own cardboard cigarette case, now contains a tiny explosive lens. With your military background you surely know what that is... When it explodes, it will produce a hole in your chest that looks a lot like the impact of a dumdum bullet..."

"You crazy bitch," Cedric muttered with a trembling voice, "What on earth are you talking about?"

"Well, if you want me to spell it out for you, right now the explosive device I'm speaking of is located in the breast pocket of your dressing gown... Bye-bye, Cedric!"

The flashlight clattered to the wooden floor. And just as she could hear the pat-patting of Cedric's hand on his chest, Daisy finally pushed the transmitter's button with her thumb and a sharp explosion cracked at the other end of the room.

The last sound that Cedric uttered was a kind of "Oug!" that reminded Daisy of the word "Auge", the German term for "eye". Daisy reflected, "That's right, Cedric, an eye for an eye," and then she sprang into action.

First she stepped over to where the firecracker sound had come from, behind the desk, the Louis XVI card table, and she leaned over the body. Taking off her right hand glove, she felt for a pulse at the carotid artery, but could find none. Now she probed the breast pocket of the dressing gown with her bare hand, so as not to bloody her glove. The pocket was torn and the device inside rather mashed, but still in one piece. Victor's Irish friend had told him that the explosive charge was "just enough to knock out the Earl's heart," but that the device would stay in one piece and should be

194

removed and taken away. Victor had told the man who the mark would be and why he had to die, but not who "the operator" would be, and certainly not that it would be a blind person. The front of Cedric's gown was soaked with blood.

Putting her hand back in the glove, Daisy patted the floor around the body as lightly as she could, and found the flashlight. She cleaned it with a handkerchief from her handbag, then stepped over to the cabinet and put it back in the drawer that still was open. She shut the drawer.

She came back to the body, picked up Cedric's right hand together with the Luger, and made sure that the grip of the weapon was still firmly nestled in his palm, his fingers closed around it, his forefinger inserted through the trigger guard. Now holding his hand and the gun in both her gloved hands, Daisy aimed the muzzle towards the breast pocket. "One dumdum bullet coming," she muttered, then releasing the safety latch and pressing down Cedric's finger on the trigger, she fired the Luger once. The empty bullet casing was automatically ejected, and clattered onto the wooden floor. Daisy left it lying where it had landed. Then she carefully lay Cedric's hand down by his side, with the Luger still in his bent fingers.

Now she proceeded to put all the light bulbs she had in her handbag back in their fixtures and switched on the desk lamp and the standing lamp. She could feel through her glove that the bulbs became hot. "Cedric would have switched the lights on before he shot himself..."

Before unlocking the door and leaving the room for the last time, Daisy closed the French window she had previously opened. Then she went up to the bedroom upstairs and also closed the window there. Finally she went down to the ground floor, reconnected the phone lines, and then all the way down to the basement, where she turned the main valve of the boiler back to normal. At last she left the house through the basement window, securing the doctored latch so that no one could see that it could be opened from the outside.

At the end of the driveway a car was waiting for her just inside the main gate. Daisy knocked softly on the roof and the driver opened the door. He briefly shone a flashlight on her. "Hullo, princess, you look like a butcher's wife: spattered with blood…"

"Of course! I almost forgot: I'm wearing my coat inside out and I must turn it back now!"

"Yes, and let me clean your face a bit with my handkerchief…"

"No, wait! Take mine… I'll have to take a bath and change my clothes before I go to the group practice."

"Of course. You'll have plenty of time for that. Get in the car."

As they drove off Daisy said, "I dropped my bomb load right on target. He didn't confess; he never apologised. Back to base now! And you, rear-gunner, any night fighters on the prowl?"

"Nothing much. A bit boring. Let's just forget we were even here."

The whole crew had been involved in the planning of tonight's operation. As Victor himself was probably known as a bookmaker and the most likely to be under scrutiny from the police, it had been decided that someone else should drive the car. All four of the crewmembers who were present had volunteered, and it was more or less on a whim that Daisy had chosen the rear gunner.

After driving through the dark for a while, Cray suddenly broke the silence.

"Listen, princess, there's something I have to tell you. This Cedric chap you just killed was a murderer, and obviously he deserved to die. But now that you killed him I feel a bit guilty, because that despicable man was not the only one who wanted Ralph dead… What I'm trying to say is:

I also wished him dead at some stage, and so did the rest of the crew."

"I beg your pardon? What on earth are you talking about!"

"Well, you see, the thing is, in those last weeks before he died we all thought that poor Ralph was losing it. Cracking up; breaking down; losing his nerve; going chicken. And *that*, we thought, was happening because of *you*... You two were so much in love and having such fun; you were so happy together, that Ralph started fearing death... He wasn't functioning properly anymore because he loved life too much, and that scared the *hell* out of us all...

"Wait a minute... does this mean that you actually distrusted Ralph... at some stage? How's that even possible?"

"Of course, with hindsight, we now know that it only *looked* as if he'd lost it, because of the arsenic poisoning. But you understand, at the time it looked real enough, so we all thought he was cracking up... We pleaded with him: get a grip, stop writing all those love letters in your diary, it makes you lose your focus, this is becoming dangerous. He obliged; he stopped writing, as you know, but it didn't help at all. He still had all the symptoms of fear."

"So that's the *real* reason why he stopped writing, not because he was feeling so sick... And *that* is what you chaps were holding back during our flight. I had a hunch you were all keeping something from me."

"I'm afraid we did, yes. You know, we even did a test, once. The engineer and the navigator started feeding him bogus figures on the way back home, one day. 'We're losing oil,' they said, 'the engines are overheating,' and on top of that 'we're way off course.' The wireless told him that we had lost contact and that we were on our own. Ralph should have prepared to bail out; at least given the order to put on the parachutes... But he wouldn't hear of it. We kept flying home and damn the consequences. Of course we made it home all right, we were fine, really, it was only a test. And Ralph laughed at us: 'You ninnies, I told you we'd be all right!' But if the crisis had been real, he would have killed us all instead of bailing out... The whole plan of ending up in a 'Stalag Luft', which had been Ralph's idea in the first place, was not going to happen with this attitude of his. And that is when we all started thinking that we needed a new skipper urgently."

"Now wait a minute!" Daisy exclaimed. "Whatever happened to the 'magic of the crew'? I thought you guys were like a married couple, extended to seven men. Weren't you supposed to stand up for your skipper no matter what?"

"Yes, yes, of course, but that's the thing, don't you understand? You have to be able to trust one another blindly. But it cuts both ways. When you lose that trust, your very life is at stake, you just can't afford to beat around the bush. You have to take action immediately..."

"What kind of action are you talking about, for Christ's sake?"

"We had already decided to go to the Commander and tell him that our skipper was losing it..."

"Good God!"

"Yes, I know... But poor Ralph died on us just before we could actually ask for his replacement. When we woke up on that fateful day and we were told that he was dead, we all felt some relief... Not only relief, of course, we were saddened by his death as well, obviously, but at least now we were going to have a new skipper. Problem solved..."

"Good God! You guys didn't tell me any of this during my flight with you to Berlin... I mean, we did discuss those last weeks and Ralph's death at length, but you said nothing about all this..."

"Well, we didn't really *lie* to you, either, did we? But it is clear that we all held back, somehow, that much is true... I guess this happened quite spontaneously, you know?"

"But then why are you telling me *now*?"

"Well, you've just killed a man tonight. It was awfully brave of you to do it yourself instead of hiring a professional killer. And you seem to be taking it like a real trooper, but it is going to hit you eventually, believe me. And I guess that in a way I'm trying to ease your burden by telling you that we all do terrible things… And also: that this Cedric deserved to die, you know? The biggest crime he committed, apart from killing Ralph, is that he made us despise and distrust our skipper. *That* is the worst part of what Cedric Clifton did… At least for me."

The next day, at the end of the afternoon, when Daisy came back from work, her neighbour Mrs Maurois was waiting for her on the landing. The old lady's front door was open and the distinctive odour of her flat hung heavily and unmistakably on the stairs.

"Hullo, Mrs Em," Daisy cried while she reached her floor. "To what do I owe the pleasure?"

"Well, sorry for barging in on you just when you're coming home from work; it's not my habit, as you know, but there's something in the newspaper that you must really hear…"

"Of course, Mrs Em, You know I'm *always* interested in the latest news, so please come in. Let's have a cup of tea together…"

Daisy unlocked her own front door and they entered her flat.

"There's a short item in the paper about Bottomleigh House, my dear Daisy. That is the manor where your dear Ralph grew up, isn't it?"

"Yes, indeed. To the manor born my Ralph was, born and bred at Bottomleigh House; so let's hear it. I'm all ears!"

And while Daisy set the kettle for tea, the old Lady read out a news report, titled "Earl Felled by Fate", to the effect that "a terrible accident", with deadly outcome, had befallen

199

the Earl of Haverford at Bottomleigh House, West Sussex. As he had been "inspecting" his collection of firearms, all of them licensed and registered, of course, he apparently did not take into account the fact that the safety latch of his Luger was not secured and that the weapon was loaded with special ammunition. The police arrived too late on the premises to reanimate the hapless victim of this terrible accident...

As Daisy handed her old neighbour a cup of tea, she remarked, "This news despatch is a deplorable piece of prose, Mrs Em. In a little more than a hundred and fifty words they repeat the expression 'terrible accident' half a dozen times, and 'deadly outcome' only once. And you know what this means, Mrs Em?"

"No. You tell me."

"It means that they are very much afraid that we might think the Earl has committed suicide."

"Good Lord, Daisy! Do you really think the man committed suicide?"

"Oh yes, it is quite possible. I knew the current Earl a little, you know. He was *not* a happy man, living all alone in that big house..."

"Good grief! Now *that* would be a piece of news, if it came out!"

"Exactly!"

"Do you know what I like about you, dear Daisy?"

"No. You tell me."

"You have an original point of view on everything..."

"Yes, there's more to me than meets the eye, don't you think?"

"Yes, indeed!"

As they sat together and sipped their tea peacefully, there was a knock at the door, which had been left ajar when the two women had entered the flat. "Hello?" a male voice cried.

"Skipper! Is that you? You're back! Do come in!"

To her old neighbour Daisy stage-whispered, "That is my new paramour, Mrs Em. May I ask you to leave us alone now?"

"Of course, darling. And he is a pilot too, just like Ralph..."

"That's right! Goodbye! And thank you for the news!" Then she flew into Rick's arms, and after they'd had a long, warm embrace, she asked happily, "When is your next flight to Rio, skipper? I think I want to take you up on your offer."

Acknowledgements

Thanks to those early readers who managed to recognize the value of a rough diamond: Hanna van der Ven, Judith Ouwehand (who also modelled for the cover) and Christopher Wainwright. To Erja Krings in particular, whose brainwave about the title was most welcome. Special thanks to Alex Hammond for his very professional assessment of the MS.

I am very much indebted to Patrick Bishop's "Bomber Boys: Fighting back 1940-1945" for background details.

Finally, many thanks to you, dear reader who bought my book. If you really liked it (or loathed it!) I'd appreciate your customer review on Amazon.

Printed in Great Britain
by Amazon